MW01135199

THREAT OF MAGIC

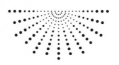

LINSEY HALL

CHAPTER ONE

Training facility at the secret Amazon warrior headquarters

The warrior lunged at me, her sword swiping for my neck.

My heart lurched as a I ducked low, avoiding her strike. I gripped my own sword, unfamiliar with the new Amazonian weapon, and whirled away from her. She growled and charged, but I was ready.

I sliced at her with my blade, narrowly missing her neck.

"It's in the wrist!" shouted Alkaia, my trainer, from the sidelines. "Don't forget the wrist."

Damn it, Alkaia was right. I was forgetting the wrist. The Amazons—some of the most famous warriors in history—were letting me train with them, and I was forgetting the damned wrist.

My opponent came at me again, wielding her xiphos with precision. *She* certainly wasn't forgetting to use her wrist, and the short sword nearly struck me.

I gripped my own xiphos and danced out of her way, my

fancy footwork the only thing saving me from getting a slice to the arm.

Because they were immortal badasses, the Amazons trained with real weapons. I had a few nasty slices to show for it.

All around, the training room bustled with people practicing their swordplay. Today, I was up against Lykopis, a warrior who was over two thousand years old but looked only twenty. She wore modern black tactical gear. Her dark hair swung in a long ponytail and her green eyes followed my every move like a snake.

I really liked Lykopis, except for the fact that she was probably going to kick my ass.

I quickstepped away from her, heading back toward the wall as I considered my options.

Speed was the only thing that could make up for my shoddy wrist-work, so I waited until she lunged for me. As her steel glittered, I darted right, going low toward her waist. I moved as quickly as I could, swiping out with my blade and striking her lightly in the side. I pulled my punches, not wanting to hurt her too badly since this was training.

She hissed, darting away from me.

Sweat dripped down my temples and I grinned.

"Enough!" Alkaia stepped forward, slicing her hands through the air. Her blonde hair hung in long waves, streaked with black to match the tactical gear that all the Amazons wore.

"Damn it." Lykopis scowled. Then she nodded and met my gaze. "Well done."

There was no bitterness or insincerity in her tone. That's what I liked about the Amazons. They made a great team. Lykopis didn't like being beaten—hell, no one did—but she was a good loser when her opponent was one of her fellow Amazons.

It still wowed me that *I* was one of them.

I'd only learned about the Amazons a week ago, but they were quick to adopt me as one of their own. I still spent most of my time at the Protectorate castle in Scotland, but I'd managed to steal over to their compound for an hour a day to train with them. The rest of my time was spent hunting for the Stryx, the evil witches who'd become my mortal enemies.

"You need to use your wrist." Alkaia's words cut through my distraction, and I turned to her.

"I know."

"Your mind is elsewhere," Alkaia said.

There was no point in telling her that my mind was on the Stryx. All the Amazons knew it. I'd spent most of the last four days hunting them, sparing only an hour for training.

"I'll try harder." I looked down at the short sword that was vaguely leaf shaped. The ancient Greek blade was unfamiliar in my hands, but I liked it.

Behind Alkaia, a set of elevator doors whooshed open. Queens Hippolyta and Penthesilea stepped out, their expressions as stern as always.

I admired the queens. They'd ruled jointly over the Amazons for over two thousand years, and under their watch, the race of ancient warriors had become some of the most successful mercenaries in the world. They fought only on the side of good, of course, but any battle they joined was won.

The queens strode toward me, each wearing identical black tactical wear. They didn't look any different than their soldiers, really, but the power that rolled off them was definitely different. These women packed a seriously powerful magical punch, and they were looking right at me.

Alkaia stepped to the side, joining me, and Lykopis disappeared toward the locker rooms.

The queens stopped in front of us. They were both tall, but it was their magic that made them seem like they towered over everyone else in the room.

"How is your training going?" Queen Penthesilea asked.

I looked down at the sword. "Good. I need to work on my wrist, but good."

"She's exceptionally talented," Alkaia said.

Heat warmed my cheeks. Alkaia wasn't full of compliments when she was training me, but I'd take them any time I could get them. She reminded me a bit of Jude, my trainer at the Academy. The stuff I did with the Amazons was on my off time, but I liked doubling up.

"We have good news," Queen Hippolyta said. "Tiresias has been spotted near the Black Sea."

"The seer?" The name rang a bell, but I'd been hunting down so many leads for powerful seers that they were getting fumbled in my head.

"The most famous seer from Ancient Greece," Queen Penthesilea said. "He's been missing for centuries—a real hermit, that one. But he's been spotted by our sources. Right in the Black Forest, near the Black Sea. By the shore, we think."

I grinned. "And he might be able to help me find the Stryx."

Both queens nodded, their smiles broad.

Four days ago, after the Stryx had released three Titans from their prison in Tartarus, all five of them had disappeared. Poof, gone, no trace.

We had no idea what they were up to, but Titans were the magical equivalent of nuclear weapons. They were giants with magical gifts to rival the gods, and we didn't know what the Stryx wanted with them. It was safe to assume that whatever it was, it'd change the world as we knew it.

And not in a good way.

As a result, everyone was on the lookout. The Protectorate was dedicating all of its manpower to finding them. Maximus, my sorta-boyfriend who considered it his life's work to make me swoon, said that the Order of the Magica was doing everything they could to find them, as well.

The Amazons were helping on the condition that I showed up at their base of operations to train for an hour a day. I was one of them, and even though I wouldn't live here like the rest, they wanted me to learn their ways. In return, they helped me hunt for the Stryx.

And this was our first real lead. A seer powerful enough to shed some light on the problem.

Queen Penthesilea dug into her pocket, then handed me a small black stone. "This will take you to the Black Forest. It is dangerous, so you must be careful. You will find Tiresias on an island in the lake."

"We suggest that you bring backup," Queen Hippolyta said. "There are dangerous things in that forest."

"I will." I gripped the transport charm tightly. "Thank you for this."

"Thank *you*, Rowan." Queen Penthesilea nodded. "You are the one fated to defeat the Stryx. We will do everything in our power to help you succeed, for the alternative is catastrophe."

Ancient queens had a tendency to speak in dramatic language, but in this case, she was right. The Stryx were as deadly as an army of giant cobras who could teleport right into your bedroom.

With those final, ominous words, the queens swept out of the room. I sighed, sagging.

"Do you need backup?" Alkaia asked.

I glanced at the clock over the bank of elevators, noticing that it was nearly four. "No. I've got just the person in mind. But thank you."

In fact, I was late for a date with him.

In fairness, the word *date* was pretty generous for what we had planned. Not that we didn't want to go on a real one, but the most we had time for these days was a quick drink while comparing notes on our hunt for the Stryx.

Alkaia nodded. "Well, good work with the xiphos. And be safe out there."

"I'll do my best." I hurried from the room, catching one of the elevators that would take me to the bottom floor of the huge building that served as the Amazon's headquarters. It looked like any of the other fancy glass buildings in Istanbul's business district, though most people had no idea what it housed.

The sun was low in the sky as I stepped outside, and I dodged left to avoid being run over by a businessman who hurried to some place that was clearly *very* important.

Maximus and I had agreed to meet at a little bar near the Amazons' building, and it didn't take me long to get there. I stepped inside the dimly lit interior and spotted him immediately.

He sat at a little table in the corner, his powerful form dwarfing the small piece of furniture. Damn, he looked good. His hair was rumpled and his eyes a bit tired, but that was par for the course with the all-out manhunt going on. Though he looked relaxed in his jeans and battered brown leather jacket, there was a coiled strength in his muscles. He could be up and fighting in the blink of an eye.

I strode toward him, weaving between the little tables and chairs. When I stopped in front of his table, his gaze rose to meet mine.

A devastatingly sexy smile dragged at the corner of his lips. "You look good."

"So do you."

"No, I mean, you look *really* good."

Warmth flushed through me. He'd noticed.

Before I'd gone to train with the Amazons, I'd changed into

my date outfit. As much as I might like the idea of a dress—something I'd really gotten a taste for at Cinderella's ball a while back—my life wasn't currently suitable for dresses.

So I'd gone for a sparkly pink top to add a bit of color to my black jeans and black leather jacket. My Mighty Magical Magenta lipstick finished the look. Honestly, not only was I a sucker for hot pink lipstick, I was a *major* sucker for ridiculous names, and Mighty Magical Magenta fit that bill perfectly.

"Thanks." I sat. "But I'm afraid I have to cancel our date."

He nodded, expression somber. "I was actually here to say the same."

For the briefest moment, an icicle of fear stabbed me. He wasn't bailing on *me,* was he? I mean, I was cancelling because we had to go hunt a seer. But him...?

He seemed oblivious to my concern though.

Men.

"Did you find something?" I asked. "Does the Order have a lead?"

The waitress interrupted then, setting two glasses on the table. Hot Turkish coffee wafted up, smelling sweet and strong. Thank fates it wasn't Raki. I definitely didn't have the time or the stomach for a hangover like my last one.

"Do you need anything else?" she asked.

I just wanted her to go away. She was prolonging my angst.

"That's fine, thank you." Maximus didn't sound like he was in any hurry.

She snapped her gum and left.

I leaned toward Maximus, brows raised. "Well?"

"There have been developments with the Titans," Maximus said.

Part of me relaxed while the other part of me tensed up like a mouse in a snake pit. "What kind?"

Nervously, I sipped my coffee.

"The Order of the Magica has a department dedicated to measuring the amount of dark magic in the world. Normally, it's relatively stable. Slight fluctuations as demons escape the hells and arrive on earth, but usually nothing we can't handle."

"Let me guess, the amount of dark magic is increasing."

"Exponentially. It increased as soon as the three Titans escaped from Tartarus, but it has continued to grow."

I shivered. "What do you mean, it's continued to grow? The Protectorate has guards on the closed entrance to Tartarus. No more of them could have escaped. It's not possible." My skin chilled. "Unless there's another exit?"

He shook his head. "We don't think so. The mages at the Order think that the Titans are growing stronger. With their ties to Tartarus broken, their magic is expanding."

"Shit." They'd already been insanely strong. As tall as houses, with magic to rival the gods.

"Their dark magic is increasing so much that it's upsetting the magical balance of the world. With so much dark magic in the air, more evil will spread. To supernaturals *and* humans."

"Wait, what do you mean?"

"If people have a devil and an angel sitting on their shoulder, the devil is about to get a lot louder. It will be like a plague that influences people to commit evil deeds. More robbery, chaos, abuse, murder. If the Titans' powers are allowed to grow unchecked, the world will fall into darkness. All of the good in people will be stamped out."

"Oh fates." I leaned back in my chair. That was *bad* news. There were already enough people out there doing evil shit. They kept the Protectorate plenty busy. But if all the good people started doing evil shit, too?

"That will turn the world into hell," I said.

Maximus nodded. "And it won't take long, according to the Order experts."

"Has it started?"

Maximus nodded sharply. "We monitor the human police radio. They're already responding to more calls. Violent ones. And black magic neighborhoods like Darklane are bustling with even more supernaturals than normal. They're drawn to the darkness."

Crap. "How long do we have?"

He shrugged. "A week? Honestly, it's hard to say. If a thousand humans without access to guns are inclined to start knife fights, it's bad. If a thousand humans with guns or access to nuclear codes are inclined to start a fight, it gets *much* worse."

So the world could be a hellscape in a week. Fantastic. "Does the Protectorate know?"

"The Order sent someone to inform them."

I nodded. "Okay, right. So we're looking at basically no time to solve a giant problem."

"The usual."

"Well, it's good I have a lead, then. The Amazons have located a powerful seer. An ancient Greek who is apparently still alive but doesn't show himself often."

"Where is he?"

"The Black Sea. Near the Amazons' original homeland." I set the transport charm on the table. "They gave me this. We can go find him."

"Right away."

I nodded and stood, picking up my coffee and throwing it back. It'd grown cold without me noticing, but I was going to need the energy. I doubted we'd have much time to rest until we saved the world. *If* we could save the world.

Maximus left a few bills on the table. Then nodded toward the door. "Shall we?"

"Let's go kick some Titan ass."

CHAPTER TWO

I stepped into the portal, allowing the ether to suck me in and send me through space. When it spat me out in the forest, I was out of breath.

All around, the trees creaked and groaned. They were black, shriveled things, so ancient that they must have seen the Amazons when they'd originally lived along the shore of the Black Sea thousands of years ago.

Maximus appeared next to me. He looked around. "This place is haunted."

I shivered, feeling it in the air. It was hard to miss. "No kidding."

I drew in a deep breath and used my super hearing, a gift from Artemis. Last week, the Greek goddess had given me some of her powers. They included the ability to command animals to my will—sort of. They didn't attack when I asked them not to, at least. I was still working on getting them to clean my house. Another perk was that I was also able to hear and see extremely well.

Though I carefully searched the forest, I picked up no signs of life. Even the trees had no leaves, and their bark was black. It was winter, but they didn't feel dormant. For all I knew, they were dead.

The sound of waves crashed in the distance. I looked at Maximus. "I can hear the Black Sea to the right. The queens said that Tiresias would live near the shore."

We made our way through the forest, our footsteps quiet on the soft ground. Occasionally, a branch would snap beneath our feet or the wind would whistle through the trees. Other than that, I sensed no signs of life.

The sound of the waves grew louder as we approached, but there was something...off.

Was that a heartbeat? "Do you hear that?"

"No." Maximus kept his voice soft and his footsteps silent.

I peered through the trees, squinting to try to catch a glimpse of anything in the dim light. Night was falling, and I prayed that we were alone in this forest.

To my right, a twig broke. The sound cracked through the evening, shockingly loud.

Maximus stiffened. "We're being followed."

I could barely hear him over the sound of the wind through the trees.

But he was right.

Someone was out there.

I kept my eyes peeled on the forest around us. When I caught sight of an animal's legs in the distance, I frowned.

Was that a goat?

Goats weren't predators.

It appeared again, darting from the shelter of one tree trunk to the next.

Nope. That was not a goat.

That was a man.

With goat legs.

He was definitely a creature straight from Greek myth, with

the legs of a goat and the top half of a man. He wore no shirt despite the fact that the night was brisk. Horns protruded from his head, but that was all the detail I could spot through the darkness. He was careful to keep the trees between himself and us. He shifted, and I caught a glimpse of his bow and arrow.

Pointed straight at us.

Another twig broke, this time on the other side of the forest. Closer to Maximus.

I swallowed hard and looked at Maximus. He nodded silently, gaze intense. The message was clear.

We were being hunted.

I reached into the ether and withdrew a shield. Maximus followed my lead, and conjured his own shield. We walked side by side through the forest, each holding our shield between us and the goat man.

Were they satyrs? Were all goat men satyrs?

There were so many elements to Greek myth that I really needed to study. But whatever he was, it was bad news.

Quietly, we continued through the forest. When the goat man stopped, I felt it more than heard it. There was a sudden stillness, and my heart began to pound. Adrenaline flooded my muscles, and I felt like prey.

No joke, I might as well have been a rabbit caught in the gaze of a fox.

"Duck!" I hissed.

I dropped to my knees, holding the shield in front of my entire body. Maximus did the same, thrusting his shield in front of me.

The arrow smashed into my shield.

I looked at Maximus. "You're supposed to protect *yourself* with your shield."

"Shields are for protecting what we find valuable."

If there'd been time for my heart to melt, it would've been in a puddle somewhere around my feet. Now was not the time, however.

"We're just trying to pass peacefully through your forest," I shouted. "We're looking for Tiresias. We need to ask him some questions."

"The prey speaks?" The goat man's voice had a strange intonation. Like he was bleating.

I'm not prey! I stood, reaching into the sack that hung over my back and yanking out a potion bomb. I raised my shield in front of my torso, and sprinted toward the goat man. I ran full out, barreling into the forest. For effect, I added a roar. The primal scream unnerved even me.

Soon, I was close enough to get a good look at him. More importantly, I had a good shot.

I raised the potion bomb, a stunner, and threw it at him. For the briefest moment, he blinked stupidly, staring at me like a moron. At the last minute, he ducked, and the bomb sailed over his head.

From behind, I could hear Maximus charge across the forest floor. Then the sound of clashing steel. I wanted to turn and watch the fight, to make sure that Maximus was okay. But there was no need. He could handle himself. And frankly, I didn't have the time. The goat man was raising his bow and arrow again.

I reached into my bag and withdrew another potion bomb. The blue glass gleamed in the light of the setting sun, and I chucked it at the goat man. He was too busy aiming his bow, and by the time he spotted the blue glass ball flying toward him, the potion bomb crashed against his chest, spraying blue liquid everywhere.

His eyes widened briefly.

"Not used to your prey attacking?" I asked. "And here I thought goats were vegetarians."

He toppled over backwards, hitting the ground with a loud thud.

I crouched low to make a smaller target of myself and searched the forest for another attacker. I could hear no one, but the hair on the back of my neck stood up. It was almost like I could feel someone in the distance off to my left.

They watched me.

They wanted to kill me.

They wanted to *eat* me.

Holy fates, the power that Artemis had given me was amazing. I'd never felt this before, but I was damned certain I'd developed the instinct of a prey animal.

It was creepy. I didn't like how it made my heart race and adrenaline fill my body. I didn't like how my skin chilled, or the hair on my arms stood on end. But I appreciated it.

This was a power that could save my life.

Slowly, I turned toward the sense of danger, reaching into my potion bag and gripping another bomb. I withdrew it, squinting through the darkness.

In the distance, the bare branches of the trees rustled. I looked up, squinting. Could a goat man climb?

Then I spotted the eyes through the tree limbs, peering down at me.

Yup. Goat men can climb.

He raised his bow and arrow, sighting it toward me.

Before he could fire, I hurled my potion bomb at him, knowing that my aim would be true. I could just feel it.

A second later, it crashed against his shoulder. With any luck, he wouldn't break his neck when he fell from the tree. I'd chosen a weaker stunner, and I wanted to grill him. The other goat man would be out for hours, but not this guy. As long as he didn't break his neck.

He hit the ground with a heavy thud. I took a moment to

survey my surroundings, but I could neither see nor sense any kind of threat. To my left, the sound of battle ceased.

"Maximus?"

"I'm fine."

"Good. I'm going to grill this one over here." I hurried toward the fallen goat man, keeping my senses alert. Just because there weren't any more threats didn't mean they wouldn't show up in a minute.

The goat man was sprawled beneath the tree, his bow and arrow scattered. Fortunately, he wore a little loincloth. If I knew one thing in this world, it was that I did not want to see a goat's dangly bits.

I knelt at his side, inspecting his fallen body. Neck looked okay, and nothing else was at a particularly weird angle.

I poked him in the shoulder. "Hey, wake up."

He groaned, and it sounded a hell of a lot like bleating.

Maximus knelt on the other side of the goat man, his blue eyes meeting mine. "What did you hit him with?"

"A light sedative. He should be sort of out of it, but still able to answer questions. As long as we can convince him to."

"That won't be a problem." Maximus conjured a small dagger, and pressed the tip to the base of the goat man's throat.

"Dude! Wake up." I shook the prostrate man's shoulder, and his eyes fluttered open.

He had no whites to his eyes, and they flickered a strange greenish brown. The pupils were slanted like a goat's. His gaze met mine.

"What the hell is your problem, dude? I thought goats were vegetarians. Why were you trying to kill us?"

"On our land." His words were garbled and slow.

"So, it's an automatic death sentence?"

He didn't answer. And honestly, I didn't care. Not really. "Do you know where Tiresias is?"

The goat man tightened his jaw, and it was pretty clear he didn't want to talk.

Maximus pressed the dagger closer to his neck, and a small bead of blood welled. "Answer the lady."

"Honestly, I'm the scary one." I grinned at the goat man, trying to make myself look crazy. It wasn't that hard.

His eyes widened. "Women should not be fighters."

I growled. "I forgot how sexist the ancient Greeks were."

Maximus nodded sagely and looked down at the goat man. "Friend, I suggest that you not say such things in the future. She objects. And when she objects, well, I don't think you want to know what happens."

I drew a dagger from the ether and twirled it in my fingers. The goat man's eyes followed the glinting steel.

I tapped it against my lips. "Now, tell me where Tiresias is. We're not gonna hurt him. But if you don't tell me, I *will* hurt you."

Frankly, the idea of hurting him while he was down like this made my stomach turn. But he didn't need to know that. Whether or not I was going to live up to my threats didn't matter as long as the threat itself was convincing.

Apparently it worked, because he opened his mouth. "There is an island near the shore. He spends time there."

"Any tricks on how to get there? Anything to look out for?" Maximus asked.

The goat man shook his head.

I wasn't sure if I believed him. Maximus didn't seem sure either. He pressed his dagger into the goat man's skin. It didn't go deep, but the goat man's eyes widened again.

"Ignore the trees," he said.

"Ignore the trees?" I frowned at him.

"That's what I said, isn't it?"

"Why?"

"Because—" The goat man choked, the words no longer able to leave his throat.

I squinted at him, then looked Maximus. "I think he's been cursed not to speak of it."

"Agreed."

This was probably as much as we were going to get out of him. "Can you conjure some rope, Maximus?"

He nodded, and his magic swelled on the air. I drew in the scent of cedar, loving the hell out of Maximus's scent. A moment later, several lengths of rope appeared on the ground next to me.

"I'll get this one," Maximus said.

"Thanks." I took a couple pieces, then hurried over to the first goat man that I'd hit with the longer-acting sedative.

Quickly, I bound his limbs. If he woke up before we were out of the forest, I didn't want to run into him again. Or his arrows.

By the time I returned to Maximus, he'd bound the semiconscious goat man and was waiting for me.

"What about the other one?"

He shook his head. "No need."

"All right, then. Let's go."

We started through the forest again, heading towards the shore. As we walked, I kept my senses alert. Dark was falling, and my night vision kicked in. It was strange, almost like I was seeing the world in black and white. But I could see almost as well as I could in the daylight now. Without question, I liked Artemis's gifts the best.

As we walked through the trees, noise floated through the leaves. Something like whispers.

I blinked, looking around. "Do you hear that?"

"The whispers?" Maximus nodded. "But what are they saying?"

I tilted my head, listening harder. At first, the noise was indistinguishable from wind. In fact, the whispers sounded so much like wind that I wouldn't have thought them out of place in a forest.

But there was something almost human about them. Like there was life to them.

And then the words became clear.

Help me.

Help me.

Help me.

I shivered, fear icing my skin. I reached for Maximus's hand.

I'd faced down demons, giants, witches, monsters. Even Titans.

But this? The sound of somebody so miserable, so in distress. *This* frightened me.

I stopped abruptly, dragging Maximus to a halt. I turned around, twisting myself to see the entire forest. I didn't let go of Maximus's hand, and he had to follow me around in a circle. He didn't let go, though, as if he knew how freaked out I was. Spiders crawled up my back, fear given form.

"Do you hear that?" I looked at Maximus.

His skin whitened. "I do now."

"Where are they?"

"I can't see them."

The only thing in the forest I could see were the trees. There weren't even bushes or scrub brush or ferns or flowers. Just trees. Ancient and dead-looking.

It sounded like the whispers were coming *from* the trees.

"The goat man said to ignore the trees." I shook my head, not liking the sound of that.

We couldn't ignore them.

Not when they were so miserable.

I let go of Maximus's hand, approaching one of the trees on shaky legs. There was something terrible here, something I didn't want to face.

Help me.

Something I *had* to face.

I raised a trembling hand and pressed it to the rough bark of the tree. It poked the tender skin of my palm. Two life forces pounded in the tree, and I gasped, jerking my hand away.

I turned back to Maximus to find that he was right behind me.

Concern shadowed his eyes. "What is it? You look like you've seen a ghost."

"Not a ghost. A possession." I turned back, studying the bark as my heart thundered in my ears. I pressed my palm to the bark again. I shuddered as two life forces bombarded me. "Someone is trapped in the tree."

"How is that possible?"

"The Greek gods did this all the time." I shook my head, disgust shooting through me. "They often turned women into trees. Usually when she incited the lust of a god and ran from him. They considered it protection for her. Better to turn her into a damned tree than tell the jerk to stop being creepy."

"What bastards." Maximus frowned. "Can we get her out?"

"We have to."

"How, though? It's not like a regular prison."

"No, it's some horrible magic that binds her to the tree." I pressed my other hand to the bark, closing my eyes. If I focused very hard, I could feel the difference between the two lifeforms. One was clearly arboreal—that was the tree. But the other—that was human.

I was going to have to use my power to suck the life out of the tree without hurting the human life. It would be like performing surgery, the hardest thing I'd ever done with my power.

Why was it that the power I hated the most was the one that could do the most good? It should be an evil gift, but somehow, when I forced myself to use it, it could do great things.

As carefully as I could, I began to draw the tree's life force out of the bark. It flowed up my arms and into my chest, seeming to suffuse my soul with its strength. But there was something almost dirty about it. Not nearly as bad as the life that I had sucked out of the Stryx, but this was a life-form that had been used to trap another. One of the gods, maybe Zeus since he was a real bastard, had given this tree a bit of his magic in order to trap whatever nymph or beautiful woman was locked in there.

Slowly the magic traveled from the tree into my body. Strength flowed through me, followed by nausea that roiled in my stomach.

As I continued to work, my knees buckled, and I nearly went to the ground.

CHAPTER THREE

Maximus gripped my waist, holding me upright. I leaned into his strength, grateful to have him here.

As my magic flowed into the tree, I began to feel the life force of the woman even stronger. It took intense concentration not to steal her energy, and I used everything I'd learned while practicing this power to keep her safe.

By the time I'd taken most of the tree's life force, the bark began to fall away. It turned to dust before it hit the ground, and I breathed shallowly to avoid drawing it into my lungs.

"I think you're almost there." Maximus kept his hands gripped around my waist as I worked, supporting me. The strength of the tree was flowing through me, but taking such icky magic made me ill.

The last of the bark fell away, revealing the shape of a woman. She was made of wood, but as I sucked the last of the power out of the tree, magic began to swirl around her form. Swoops of gold floated around her, sparkling and bright.

The magic flared, and the woman gasped. When the light faded, I blinked.

The tree was gone, and in its place stood a beautiful woman.

She was so gorgeous it almost hurt to look at her.

"Thank you." She gripped my arm, her emerald eyes gleaming. Her flame-red hair was bright despite the darkness, and if she needed a job in modern day, I was 1000 percent certain that she could be a swimsuit model.

"Who are you? How did you become trapped in the tree?" I ran my gaze up and down her body, making sure there were no wounds or any part of her that was still made of wood.

Thank fates, but she looked whole and healthy.

"Apollo was chasing me, and he would not cease. Nothing could make him stop. To save me, my father, Peneus, the river god, trapped me within that tree."

"Are you Daphne?"

She nodded. "How did you know?"

"You're pretty famous."

"Not for the right reasons." She scowled. "Famous for becoming a tree. The gods are bastards. Even my father."

"Bastards is right." I squeezed her arm, hoping the gesture was comforting. She seemed to appreciate it.

"Why did the goat man tell us to ignore the trees?" Maximus asked.

Her scowl deepened. "Those bastards? They're called the Panes. You can't trust a single word from their lips. They liked having us trapped in this forest."

"They were jerks." I looked around the forest. "Are there more of you in here?"

Daphne pointed to a twisted tree about twenty yards away. "Lotus is in there."

"Can you speak to her? Tell her what I'm going to do?"

"I don't need to. She knows what you're going to do. We could communicate while we were trees. Once I figured out that you were saving me, she became very excited as well."

"I don't blame her." Anger at Peneus seeped through me.

"Being trapped in there for two thousand years sounds awful."

"Longer than that." Worry creased her brow. "I don't know what I will do now, though. My whole life is gone. Everyone I knew is dead."

"I'm so sorry."

She shrugged, though her face still looked sad. "I didn't have any close family. And a few thousand years is long enough to ease the sting of losing your friends. But what will I do now?"

"We can help you," Maximus said. "I came from the past as well. Transitioning isn't easy, but this is a better world than the one you left behind."

"As long as no one thinks it's acceptable to turn me into a tree to save me from rape, I'll consider it an improvement." Daphne's eyes drifted down my form, taking in my pants. "And I can see that fashion has changed." She grinned. "I think I like it."

"I work for a place called the Protectorate. They'll help you. But first, let's get Lotus out of that tree."

This time, it was a little bit easier to separate the tree from the woman trapped within. *Practice, practice, practice, yada yada yada.* But it really did work.

I was now nearly bursting with the dark energy from the trees, but damned if this wasn't working.

When the last of the bark crumbled away, turning to dust, the figure of Lotus was revealed. The golden magic swirled around her, just like it had with Daphne, and within moments, another beautiful woman stood before me. She, too, was so gorgeous it was almost hard to look at her.

"Daphne!" Lotus threw her arms around Daphne, and the two hugged tightly. When they finally stepped apart, Lotus turned to me and threw her arms around me as well. "Thank you. Thank you so much."

"Yeah, any time." I might have conflicting feelings about my power, and about the gods who'd given them to me, but there was no denying that they were handy. And I enjoyed using them to help people. The warm glow that filled me was just icing on the cake.

Daphne turned her bright green eyes toward me. "Why are you in this miserable forest?"

"We're looking for Tiresias. We have a serious problem, and we hope he can help us."

"He can," Daphne said. "He's the best seer in all of Greek history. And I believe he has returned to this forest."

"He passed by here only a few days ago." Lotus turned to look toward the sound of crashing waves. We had to be close now. "There's a small island right off the shore, and he likes to go there. About once every one hundred years, he passes right by our trees, headed that way."

"Do you have any advice for how to reach him?" Maximus asked.

I already knew that we could trust them more than the Panes.

"The water is full of ghosts." Lotus's blue eyes glinted with fear. "Do not dwell on the past as you cross. It can devour you."

I shared a glance with Maximus. If the water was enchanted to show us our pasts—the pasts that we should not dwell upon —then we were both in trouble. Between the two of us, we had plenty of ghosts and terrible memories.

"Thank you." I smiled at them. "I'm going to call the Protectorate, the place where I live and work. They will send someone here to help you." I knew that I could speak for them without asking. This was literally in the definition of their mission statement. To help those who needed help, and two women who had been trapped in trees for thousands of years definitely qualified.

Relief relaxed the features of the two women, and they reached out to clasp hands.

I pressed my fingertips to the comms charm at my throat,

and the magic flared to life. "Ana? Bree? Can you talk?"

"Yeah, I just finished my shift at the portal to Tartarus." Ana's voice drifted out of the comms charm.

Daphne and Lotus gasped, their eyes going wide. "Tartarus?" they whispered in unison.

I nodded. "I'll explain later."

"What do you need?" Ana asked.

"I'm in the forest near the Black Sea, and I have two women here who need help from the Protectorate. Can you come pick them up? Or send someone?"

"Yes, right away. I'll follow the tracking charm that you have. I just have to get the transportation charms, and I'll be there soon."

"Thanks, Ana." The connection cut, and I turned to Daphne and Lotus.

Daphne leaned toward me, her face pale. "Tell us more about the Titans. They're *evil*."

"We need Tiresias's help because two witches, the Stryx, have released three of the Titans from Tartarus. We need to find them and put them back before the world falls into chaos."

Lotus nodded, expression grave. "Their dark magic is polluting the world, isn't it?"

"Exactly," Maximus said. "And it's working quickly."

"It would." Lotus shook her head, her face now as pale as Daphne's. "The gods imprisoned the Titans in Tartarus for several reasons, but that was the biggest one. Their magic was just too dark for the earth. It caused death and misery and chaos."

"That's what we're trying to stop," Maximus said.

"And the gates to Tartarus?" Daphne asked. "Are they closed?"

"They're closed. Don't worry."

"And your sister is one of those guards." Lotus nodded. "I

hope she's strong."

"Amazingly strong."

While we waited for Ana to show up, I answered some of their questions about the modern world. When Ana finally arrived, Daphne's and Lotus's eyes were as wide as the full moon.

Ana stepped forward, holding out her hand. "Hey, I'm Ana. I hear you need some help."

"Just a bit," Lotus said.

Daphne stepped toward Ana. "Let's leave quickly. I never want to see this forest again."

Ana saluted, then turned to me. "Do you need anything?"

"No, we've got it." I hugged her tightly, then stepped back. "Any developments back at the Protectorate?"

"No, we're still hunting for them, but none of our leads panned out."

"Be careful."

We said goodbye, and Ana took the nymphs back to the Protectorate.

I turned to Maximus. "Ready to do this thing?"

"Let's face the past." Maximus reached for my hand and squeezed.

Suddenly, the idea of facing my demons didn't sound so bad.

We made our way through the forest on silent feet, and I kept my hearing alert for any more whispering from the trees. Fortunately, we heard nothing. When we arrived at the shore of the lake, the waves were crashing gently. Moonlight glittered on the water, and it looked so peaceful. So beautiful. Could this water really be full of the ghosts of my past?

It had to be an exaggeration, right?

I pointed toward an island about half a mile from the shore. Small trees covered it, and a wisp of smoke seemed to float up from them. "That's got to be it."

I dug into my pocket and withdrew the tiny dragon scale that Ladon had given me. I laid it on the ground and stepped back, watching as the magic swirled around the little scale, and it replicated itself until it formed a beautiful boat.

I grinned and looked Maximus. "It never gets old."

He nodded and raised his hand, his magic swelling on the air. The scent of cedar and the sound of a crashing waterfall swept over me. A moment later, two oars appeared next to the boat.

I grinned at him. "Perfect. I really need to see about stashing two oars in the ether."

I'd meant to do it, but hadn't had a chance. It was expensive to buy the spell that stored something in the ether, and Bree had to ask her contact to do the work. We'd both been so busy with the Protectorate that it just hadn't happened.

The boat floated right at the edge of the beach, the waves rocking it back and forth. I used my power over the water to calm the waves, and we both climbed in. I grabbed an oar, and Maximus did the same. We used them to push the boat off the shore. The water welcomed us, rocking our little boat gently.

Maximus held out his hand for my oar, and I handed it over. Though the boat did not come with the oars, it had two handy little indents where you could prop them. Maximus began to row, his strength pulling the boat along quickly. The air was chilly here, the breeze stronger. I avoided looking down into the water, but it called to me.

I resisted, using every ounce of strength I had to look away. Instead, I looked toward Maximus.

He kept his gaze high on the horizon, his jaw tight.

Neither of us wanted to look into our pasts.

We were halfway to the island when I heard it. The sound started as whispers, sending shivers over my skin that felt like spiders crawling.

Maximus's brow tightened. He heard it, too.

What were the whispers saying?

I couldn't tell. I strained my ears, using the animal senses that Artemis had given me. Soon, it became obvious that they were calling to me. Commanding that I look at the water.

I resisted at first, my will strong. But it was almost as if the whispers were imbued with magic. The pull was magnetic. Impossible to resist. Though I fought it with every ounce of strength, my muscles burning, I couldn't avoid it forever. My gaze was forced downward, like I'd lost all control of my neck.

In the depths of the water, an image shimmered. The Rebel Gods. There was the ancient horned one, the woman covered in blood, and the one made of gold. I had been in such a magically induced stupor during my captivity with them that I'd hardly known them. They'd tried damned hard to ruin my life, though, using me for their evil plots.

Fear surged through me, along with the memory of helplessness. Anger followed quick on their heels, surging through me like molten lava.

Though my memories of that time were hazy, the feelings were not.

It was the helplessness that was the worst. It made me feel like I was drowning. Like the Black Sea was reaching up to capture me.

I gasped for breath, trying to get control of myself.

You are strong. You're not alone.

The voice whispered through me, and I swore it was my magic, speaking to me.

You are strong. You're not alone.

There it was again.

And it was right, gods damn it. I was strong. I had the magic of the gods now, and I would never be a victim again. Not only that, but even without the magic of the gods, I had been successful. I'd become a potions expert, harnessing what little magic I had to make it possible. And I'd dealt with my demons.

I was no longer that scared, trapped girl. I never would be again.

I dragged my gaze away and looked at Maximus. He stared down into the water as he rowed, his face pale, his jaw tight. The tendons stood out at his neck. Whatever he saw in the water, it was bad. Given the years that he'd spent in the Colosseum, forced to kill, his memories were probably worse than mine.

He could remember them, after all.

I had my fuzzy memories of fear and helplessness. But graphic memories would be far worse.

I reached out, and gripped his knee. My touch seemed to anchor him. He shook his head and turned his blue gaze to me. Our eyes locked. His jaw relaxed, and so did his neck. The haunted expression in his eyes faded.

Something connected us, something almost tangible. I could feel my link to him. Like a rope bound us together. I clung to it, focusing on him instead of the past, and he did the same.

It had never been so apparent that we were stronger together than apart.

Our magical skills complemented each other. We fought well together. But it was this...this ability to be an anchor in the storm for the other... That was the true strength of our relationship. We might have known each other only a short time, but it was so obvious. So obvious that it scared me.

He was the one for me. Forever. Like Cade for Bree, and Lachlan for Ana. Maximus was my one.

Did that mean I loved him?

I blinked.

It probably did. I'd never loved a guy before. I had no idea what it felt like. But I liked how this felt.

Now wasn't the time to say it, though.

We were nearly to the island, and we had a lot in front of us before there would be any time for a real date, much less expressions of love or questions about the future.

I shivered at the idea and thrust the thought away.

I kept my gaze glued on the shore, focusing on the task ahead. "We're almost there."

Maximus turned to look behind him as he rowed. He steered us toward a flat part of the beach that was nestled between two large rocks. When the boat beached itself on the shore, he jumped out and dragged the thing onto the sand. Once it stopped, I climbed out. As soon as I departed, the boat folded in on itself until it was a tiny dragon scale once more. I picked it up and put it in my pocket.

I turned, tilting my head to catch the rustle of the trees. Unlike the forest we had just left, these trees had leaves. They looked alive, and there were animals in these woods. I could sense them, could hear their heartbeats and the pad of their paws on the ground.

"Let's go." I started away from the beach, headed toward the forest.

We made our way quickly between the trees. None of the animals bothered us, but a few of them stopped to look, peeking little heads out of their dens and peering around tree trunks.

As I walked, I shifted uncomfortably. The energy from the prison trees was still bursting inside me, and I didn't love it.

When we came upon the clearing, I spotted the little house immediately. It was a cottage, something hand-built hundreds of years ago. Two thin wisps of smoke escaped from the chimney, but not enough to be from a full fire.

"Twenty bucks he's in there," Maximus said.

"I hope you're right." Because it looked pretty empty to me. Not a single light in the window, and the nearly dead fire weren't good signs.

We approached the door and stopped on the doorstep.

An intensely strong scent of rotten *something* wafted toward me. I wrinkled my nose, looking down at the ground, toward where the scent seemed to come from. A fluffy bush sat at the doorstep, reeking profusely.

"Ugh, Wither Wort." I pinched my nose. "It always reeks so badly, but it's so useful in potions."

Maximus's jaw was tight as he knocked on the door. We waited. My heart began to pound as the silence went on.

"There was a fire in the hearth. Do you think he's gone?" Maximus asked.

I tilted my head, listening. "No. I feel like I can hear his heartbeat." I strained my ears, using my new power. Yes, that was definitely a heartbeat. "He's in there."

Maximus reached for the door handle and slowly twisted. He pushed the door open, and stale air rushed out. It carried the faint scent of the fire, but mostly dust and neglect.

I darted in front of Maximus, stepping into the darkened space. Fiery red embers sat in the hearth, recently extinguished. The room was small and dimly lit by the fire with a little kitchen on one side. It wasn't much more than a table and some bowls. On the other side was a ratty old dining set. A bed lined the back wall. A figure lay on top of it.

A very still figure.

He looked like he wasn't even breathing, but I'd heard a heartbeat.

I crept toward the bed, silent as a mouse. As I neared the man, I realized that he looked so old, he might as well be a mummy. There was no fat on him, no muscle. He was made of papery skin and bones, and he lay so still that it looked like he'd been entombed here.

I couldn't even see his chest move.

My heart thundered. Oh fates, had our lead just died?

31

CHAPTER FOUR

Maximus looked at me. "Something's wrong."

I bent over the body of the too-still man and pressed my fingertips to Tiresias's slender neck. I waited, breathless.

Finally, I heard the faintest heartbeat. Even weaker than before, since I had to get this close to hear it. I looked up "He's alive. Barely."

I laid my hand upon the man's bony chest. He lay beneath a very thin blanket. Was he ill? Had someone been caring for him and left? Because he looked so bad, I would've sworn he was dead.

I focused on the life force that I felt within him, using my most useful and most hated tool. It was faint, so faint that I didn't think he'd be able to rouse himself.

What he needed was more energy.

Jackpot.

I had so much energy from the trees I'd killed to save Daphne and Lotus that I was desperate to get rid of. It swelled within me, still straining at my insides, seeming to make my skin feel tight.

"I'm going to try something." I began to push my magic into

the man, giving him the energy that I'd taken. At first nothing happened, but then I felt it. The energy was draining from me and going into him. A grin stretched across my face. I couldn't help it.

Now *this* was cool. I was like a vessel for the magical energy, able to pass it from one thing to the other if I didn't want to use it for myself.

"Are you doing what I think you're doing?" Maximus leaned closer.

"I think I am, and it's awesome." This was a rare magical skill, and I couldn't believe that I now had it. It seemed that the power of Hades was developing within me, just like Artemis's power. In a sense, I was able to give life.

Beneath my hand, the man's chest began to swell. It felt like muscles and fat were developing on top of his bones. The signs of life that had disappeared from his body were coming back.

Color returned to his face, and his cheeks filled out. His hair started to look fuller. It gleamed in the very dim light of the fire's embers.

I was definitely bringing this guy back to life.

Heck yeah.

Once I'd given him all the magic I'd taken the trees, he looked like he was just sleeping. No longer dead, just resting.

I shook him gently. "Hey, Tiresias. Wake up."

He didn't move. I shook him again.

Nothing.

I looked at Maximus. "Can you go get some of that smelly plant from outside? I think he needs something to really rouse him."

Maximus nodded. "On it."

He only needed a minute to retrieve the plant, and I took the rustic version of smelling salts from him. I waved the leaves beneath Tiresias's nose. At first, nothing happened. Then he gasped coughed, and sputtered. He sat upright, eyes wide and unseeing.

"Who's there?" he demanded.

"I'm Rowan. Can't you see me?"

"No. I'm blind, you daft fool."

"Oh, is that...normal?"

"Normal ever since that bastard Zeus took my sight." His blind eyes searched the room. "Someone else is here. Who is it?"

"I'm Maximus. We're here to ask you some questions."

"Of course you're here to ask me questions. I'm the world-famous seer, aren't I?"

"Does that mean you'll answer our questions?" I asked hopefully.

"Depends on what you give me."

"I brought you back to life tonight."

"I wasn't dead. I was just resting."

"It looked like a very deep sleep," Maximus said.

"Well, I'm 3000 years old. Of course it was a deep sleep."

There was something weird about the way this guy slept, if he started to look dead every time he did it. But that wasn't the question I wanted to ask him. I wasn't going to waste them. These seers could be tricky, and I didn't want to lose any of my chances.

"What do you want?"

Tiresias frowned. "I don't know. I have everything I want."

"How about the world? You can play a role in saving it." Maximus leaned forward. "The Titans have escaped. Three of them. We're trying to put them back, but we need to know where they are. We need to know where the Stryx are, too. Do you know anything about this?"

Tiresias scowled. "The Stryx, you say?"

"You know them?" I gripped his arm. "Please, tell me anything you know."

"Who said I know anything about that?"

"Don't play coy. You clearly know who they are."

"Fine, I hate those witches. They're evil. I'm no saint myself, but they're evil incarnate."

"Then you can help us," I said.

"I suppose I can. But first, tell me who your people are."

"My people?"

"Yes, your people. I need to know who I'm working with. I need to know I can trust you, and the best way to know somebody is to know who they associate with."

Fair enough. "I'm a student at the Undercover Protectorate Academy. My purpose there is to help the world. To protect it. To protect everyone."

"I'm not sure they deserve it." Tiresias frowned. "After you see the things I've seen, for thousands of years...Well, I'm just not sure."

"I know. There are some bastards out there. But a lot of people are good. And those are the ones I'm trying to help. Can you imagine the damage the Titans would do?"

He nodded. "Yes. In my visions, I've seen them returning to earth. They'll destroy everything good just by existing. Their black magic will pollute the world and suck all the good away."

"Not to mention whatever the Stryx have planned for them," I added.

He nodded, then turned his blind gaze to Maximus. "And who are your people?"

"I was once a gladiator in Rome, but now I work freelance for the Order of the Magica and the Undercover Protectorate. "

"Oh, another do-gooder, are you?"

"I don't know about that." Maximus shrugged. "I just know I don't want to be an asshole."

"Well, saving the world will help you avoid that fate." He turned to me. "You, girl. You said you work at the Undercover

Protectorate like this man here. Well, I'd like access to the libraries. For a full day?"

"Yes, I can arrange that."

"Do it now. I want to hear that you have permission." His wrinkled face twisted with suspicion.

It was nice to have the resources of the Protectorate behind me, that was for sure. I pressed my fingertips to my comms charm and called Bree. It didn't take long for her to find Florian and gain permission from the night librarian.

Satisfied, Tiresias nodded, and I cut the connection.

"Can you help us now?" I asked.

"I can." Tiresias led us out of the little cottage, his steps surprisingly spry for such an old man. Then again, he wasn't just any old man. Immortal Greek seers played by different rules. He also had all that energy I'd given him.

The clearing was quiet, with the moon overhead shining a bright light that illuminated the trees. Tiresias went to the center of the clearing, where the remains of a fire lay cold and black. There was a small pile of fresh wood next to it, and Tiresias began to build a fire. It didn't take him long, and soon the crackling warmth lit up the night.

Maximus and I joined him, looking down at the flickering flames.

Tiresias looked up at us, somehow able to easily find us despite his blindness. In fact, his lack of vision didn't seem to slow him down at all.

"You say that you want to know where the Stryx are located?"

"Yes." I nodded.

"Then I will need to borrow your eyes."

My jaw slackened. "My eyes?"

"What precisely do you mean by that?" Maximus asked.

"My two primary strengths as a seer are augury and seeing prophecy in the flames. Both of those skills require eyes."

"Augury?" I asked.

"Reading the future in the movement of birds. You can see how I'd need your eyes for that." He chuckled, possibly at the bad pun.

I raised a hand to my face, touching the corner of my eye. "Would you need to keep them for long? Will it hurt? Can you even put them back in?" My stomach turned. I was willing to do a lot for this cause. Anything, really. Even this. But it sounded downright *awful*.

Maximus stepped forward. "I'll do it."

Tiresias smiled. "Slow down now. I need *her* sight. She's connected to the Stryx, so it will make my vision clearer."

I swallowed hard and nodded. "What do I need to do?"

"First, we will sit." He lowered himself to the ground and crossed his legs.

I sat next to him, with Maximus on my other side.

Tiresias held out his hand, and I took it, wincing at the cold of his flesh. He turned his blind gaze to meet mine. "This will be temporary, but unpleasant. I won't be taking your actual eyes, but your ability to see."

I *really* hoped he was telling the truth.

"Okay. Do it." My voice was firm, at least.

Magic sparked around our joined hands, pale blue and bright. Under the glow of the moon, it looked like fairy lights. I could feel the animals in the forest around us, their heartbeats echoing in my ears and their footsteps growing louder as they moved closer to watch.

The blue glow traveled up my arm, and my heart began to pound. It was getting closer to my eyes. Soon, it was up toward my neck. The glow was bright, nearly blinding. I clenched my jaw, determined not to make a sound.

Maximus gripped my other hand, and I clung to him. I didn't want to rely on his support, but I wasn't strong enough to resist it.

The light glowed brighter and brighter around my body, until finally, my vision went dark.

I swallowed hard. "It's working."

"Excellent." I could hear the grin in Tiresias's voice.

Oh, fates.

I really hoped I hadn't been taken for a ride. Would he just get up and run off with my vision? I couldn't even properly race after him. I'd seen blind people accomplish incredible things. But that took practice. And right now, I was floundering as the world went dark beyond my eyes.

"Is it working?" I asked. "Can you see?"

"I can."

"You are fearless," Tiresias said. "Most would not give up their sight."

"A worthy cause." I'd seen worse things and kept going. I wasn't going to be held back. Not after so long in captivity.

"He's moving his hands over the fire," Maximus narrated. "Red magic is flowing from his palms into the flames."

"Thank you." I squeezed his hand.

Maximus continued to narrate as Tiresias made the flames dance. I felt the flicker of heat, and slowly my hearing seemed to become even better. When Tiresias shifted next to me, I felt like I could imagine exactly how he moved.

Even so, I felt my lack of sight keenly. Anxiety crawled across my skin as I waited for answers. All around, I could hear the animals as they sat at the edge of the clearing. Their feet shifted on the leaves, their hearts pounded, their fur rustled.

How many were there? Were any dangerous?

I so wanted to see them.

But I could feel them, at least. A connection that I couldn't deny. It was stronger than it had ever been. Even stronger than when I'd been with Artemis.

"The flames are flickering higher," Maximus said. "Twelve feet. Fourteen. The smoke is curling and black."

Oh, how I wish I could see.

The connection with the animals strengthened. Rabbits, foxes, wolves. I could feel them as if they were one with me. As if their hearts beat alongside my own. As if their breaths flowed with mine and their muscles moved as mine moved.

I blinked blindly.

What the heck is happening?

Because something was definitely happening. I could feel the magic between the animals and me.

My heart began to race, thudding violently in my chest. My breath heaved, and I tightened my grip on Maximus's hand.

"What is it?" he whispered, clearly able to feel my distress.

"I don't know." Then my soul left my body.

Or something.

It was impossible to describe. But one moment, my consciousness was within my own head. Then, in the next, I was joined to something new. Something feral.

I blinked, suddenly able to see.

My vision was strange at first. Colors looked different. I was lower to the ground. And damned if I wasn't looking *at myself.*

I could see myself sitting on the ground between Maximus and Tiresias, the light of the tall fire glowing red upon our faces.

Holy fates!

What was I?

I looked down, spotting big furry paws. They were gray, with long, sharp claws. I turned around and looked behind me, spotting a gray tail. The world smelled different, too. Earthier. And my thoughts were slower.

Don't stress out. Romeo's voice sounded from beside me.

I looked over, spotting the little racoon, along with Eloise and Poppy. The badger and possum stared at me with big eyes.

You're joined with the wolf. Romeo grinned toothily. *I can sense you in there.*

I tried to speak, but couldn't. This had better be temporary.

Romeo patted my leg. *You'll be fine. Just don't eat us, okay?*

I shook my head, since it was the only way I could communicate, then turned back to the fire. My body looked fine, at least. I was sitting upright and still breathing. Still holding on to Maximus's hand. That had to be a good sign. Because as cool as this power was, I didn't want to be a wolf forever.

I wanted to give a little yip and tell Maximus I was here, but I didn't dare interrupt Tiresias. Now that I could see, it was obvious that he was working hard. I didn't want to distract him from controlling the flames.

The fire flickered tall and bright, rising almost thirty feet in the air as a narrow column. Bright reds and oranges danced in the night, lighting up the trees that surrounded the clearing.

Tiresias looked up at it, his eyes darting over the flames as if he were reading a novel. Maybe he was, in a way. Seeing the future in the dance of the flames.

Thick black smoke curled up from the fire, and the sound of birds cawing echoed from it. The smoke twisted and turned, forming large black birds that rose into the sky. Hundreds of them. Moonlight gleamed off the tops of their feathers while firelight shined on them from below. They looked like sparkling gems in the night sky, and as they moved, they began to form a shape.

I squinted up at them.

What were they supposed to be?

The shape of a woman formed, and she carried two torches in her hands. Behind her, the shape of two dogs emerged. The birds continued to fly, forming a perfect pattern of the woman. I glanced down toward Tiresias, catching sight of his smile.

He seemed to recognize her.

I took a tentative step forward, wanting to nudge him into explaining what was going on. Maximus was narrating the scene to my body, seeming not to notice that I had left it.

I stared hard at my human self, trying to see if I appeared weird at all.

I didn't.

"You can come back now." Tiresias looked toward me.

Maximus eyed him, confused. Tiresias pointed at me, and Maximus's gaze followed his gesture. I gave a little yip then, and Maximus frowned.

It was time to return to my body. I'd seen what I'd needed to see, thanks to this wolf and Artemis's ever-growing magic.

I closed my eyes and imagined my consciousness returning to my human body. Though I had no idea if this would work, it seemed worth a try.

At first, nothing happened. I concentrated harder, imagining being human. Seeing through my own eyes. It took a while, but eventually the magic sparked within me. When I opened my eyes, I was once again blind.

My breath caught in my throat, and I turned toward where Tiresias was sitting. "Are we done?"

"We are."

Magic sparked around my hand, and slowly, a blue light began to glow in the darkness of my missing vision. A moment later, I could see. I peeked over toward the woods where the wolf had been standing. He was still there, but the Menacing Menagerie were gone. Smart.

"What just happened to you?" Maximus asked.

"I joined the wolf's consciousness. I'll explain more in a bit." I turned toward Tiresias, who looked right at me. His gaze was unfocused again, and I felt a bit bad about taking my sight back from him.

He looked content, however. And he sounded pleased when

he spoke. "You will need to seek Hecate. The Stryx worship her, and she will know where they are."

"Hecate? The goddess of magic?" I asked.

"And of the night, ghosts, and necromancy," Tiresias said.

"She sounds like a load of fun," Maximus said.

I cracked a smile. "I suppose the Stryx wouldn't worship anyone nice. But where do we find her?"

"She resides in the Underworld, as Persephone's companion. But it will not be an easy journey."

I frowned. The only way I knew to get into the Underworld was through Tartarus, and there was no way we were going to open up that hole again. "Do you know how to get into the Underworld?"

He shook his head. "There are several entrances, though not all are open now. You will have to find one that works."

"Do you know where any of them are?" Maximus asked.

"There was once one at Lake Avernus near Naples, Italy, and another at the ancient town of Tenarus. A third in the Alcyonian Lake at Lerna. But I don't know which ones are still open."

"We'll figure it out. Is there anything else you can tell us?"

"Best be careful. It is a deadly journey to the Underworld."

A deadly journey to the Underworld? I just hoped he didn't mean that literally.

CHAPTER FIVE

We used a transport charm to get back to the Protectorate. On the way up to the castle, I explained my adventure with the wolf, and Maximus agreed that my powers were growing.

Once inside, it didn't take long to gather the group for a meeting. Fortunately, Ana was back from her shift guarding the entrance to Tartarus. Though Bree was gone, Jude was at the castle. We agreed to meet in the library, since we had some research to do.

Jude and Ana hadn't arrived yet, and the library flickered with warm firelight as I entered the book-filled space. It was like a fantastic cavern, full of thousands of beautiful leather-bound books. They were all different colors, each of them lovingly cared for. The squashy armchairs in front of the fire beckoned, but I took a seat at the big wooden table in the middle.

Maximus joined me, looking around at all the books, an awed expression on his face. "I'll never get over this place."

"Amazing, right?"

"Truly."

"Not a lot of books in ancient Rome, I suppose?"

"None at all. Only scrolls. And there weren't many of those.

Not for a slave, at least. I only ever saw parts of an old copy of *The Odyssey*."

I nodded, grateful to live in the modern day. I reached for his hand and squeezed, delighting in the casual contact.

"That one might come in handy, though. Didn't Odysseus go to the Underworld?"

"He did."

The Pugs of Destruction lazily raised their heads from their spots in front of the fire and stared at me. Mayhem, Ruckus, and Chaos were a staple here, and I loved them from their tails to their horns. Or horns, in Chaos's case. Wings for Mayhem.

Florian, the ghostly night librarian, drifted out from the shelves, appearing right through the books. His curly white wig rose tall on his head, and his fancy coat made him look like he was about to head to a ball. He grinned widely when he saw me, and I counted my blessings that it was nighttime. Had we come in the day, we would have gotten Potts, the day librarian. True, he was alive, whereas Florian technically was not, but he was also a grumpy old bugger and I liked to avoid him.

"Here again so soon?" He drifted up to the table, his grin wide.

"Yes, we need some help figuring out which entrance to Hades is still open."

"Ah, yes." He nodded. "I've got quite a lot of firsthand accounts about trying to reach Hades. They're quite old, but one of them will have something."

"We need to meet with Jude and Ana when they arrive, but once we're done, we can help."

He waved his hand dismissively. "Oh, I've got it under control."

"Never doubted it for a second."

He gave a pleased bow and drifted away. Mayhem fluttered

up from her spot by the fire, little wings carrying her chubby ghost body high. She yipped.

"Yes, of course you can help, Mayhem," Florian said.

She flew after him.

I turned toward the library entrance just in time to see Ana enter. Her cheeks were flushed and her hair messy. She carried four paper sacks in her hands.

"Did you find something?" she asked as soon as her gaze met mine.

"Yes."

"Good." She sat and tossed a sack to Maximus and me. "Courtesy of Hans."

My stomach grumbled at the mention of the cook's name. I hadn't realized how hungry I was. I tore into the bag as she did the same. Maximus had better manners, but that was par for the course. I didn't like to let anything get between me and food.

We chomped into the sandwiches—ham and cheese—and chewed silently for a moment. Muffin, Ana's hairless winged cat, sauntered into the library. A little green jewel gleamed in his ear, a memento of his cat burglar days. Ana handed him a piece of ham from her sandwich.

By the time I polished off my sandwich, Jude had arrived. She looked exhausted, with heavy circles under her starry blue eyes. Her dark braids were pulled back from her face and her clothes looked like they needed a good wash.

Not a surprise, given that we were up shit creek.

She sat with a sigh. "Tell me you have good news."

Ana pushed the fourth paper bag at her, and Jude looked down at it like it was entirely unfamiliar.

"It's food, and you should eat it," Ana said.

"Of course." Jude unwrapped the sandwich, and I had a distinct feeling that she hadn't eaten in at least twenty-four hours. The leader of the Paranormal Investigative Team was the de facto leader of the Protectorate when dangerous things like this went down. Even though there were five heads of department, she bore the heaviest burden when things hit the fan. She took it seriously, too. "What have you got for me?"

"We spoke to a seer—Tiresias—who has told us we must go to Hades to find Hecate. The Stryx worship her, and she'll know where they are."

Jude nodded, her expression clearly impressed. "Tiresias. He's quite well-known for the accuracy of his prophecies."

"Exactly." I turned to Ana. "You crossed the River Styx once. Do you know how to get into Hades?"

She shook her head. "No. I crossed the river in Dante's Inferno. It flows from the Underworld to the Inferno—or maybe it's the other way around. Anyway, I don't know which way you should go on the river."

"That'll take too long, then," Maximus said.

"Florian is looking for a proper entrance," I said. "One that still works after all these years."

"I actually know someone who might be able to help, though," Ana said. "Nix, the FireSoul. I've heard she's been to the Greek realm of the gods."

"Really?" I didn't know Nix as well as my sisters did, given the fact that they'd met the FireSouls while I was still in captivity.

"Let me call her." Ana stood. "Be right back."

She left the room, and I looked at Jude. "How's it going at the gate to Tartarus?"

"Fine. No sign of the Stryx, and the Order of the Magica is working on solidifying the gate with magic."

"The Order has informed you of the Titans' growing dark magic?" Maximus asked.

She nodded. "They have. We're working together to create a weakening spell that will stop their magic from expanding. It

46

will debilitate them enough that we can deploy a binding spell. Once bound, they'll be helpless, and we can throw them back into Tartarus." Her expression turned serious. "If you can find them, we can stop them. We're counting on you."

"We'll find them," I said.

Maximus nodded. "Have you had any luck tracking the source of the dark magic?"

"We haven't. And we don't know how their power is growing, or what they intend to do with it all." She looked disgusted with herself. "We assume it's because they aren't bound in Tartarus anymore, but we just don't know."

It was the million-dollar question that ate at me. What the heck were they planning with all that magic?

Ana sailed back into the room. "Speaking of getting into hell, I have our expert here."

Nix entered behind her. She was a slender woman with dark hair and flashing green eyes. Her blue T-shirt was decorated with a cartoon cat, which was a nice contrast to the beat-up motorcycle boots she wore. The FireSoul was immensely powerful, though you wouldn't have known it from looking at her. She lived in Magic's Bend with Cass and Del, her two best friends and fellow FireSouls.

She grinned as she spotted me. "Rowan. Maximus. Good to see you."

"Hey, Nix. Thanks for coming."

Maximus nodded in greeting. They'd met each other at the end of the last battle, though only briefly.

She sat at the table, and her gaze met mine, suddenly turning serious. "So, you need to get into Hades?"

"We do. Do you know how?"

"I know how not to," she said.

"What do you mean?"

"I assume you need to sneak in? That you don't want to alert

Hades or Persephone or any of the other gods? Because if you do, they might want to know why you are there. And that could become a problem for you."

"Sneaking in is best. We don't need any of the wrong gods slowing us down or taking issue with us being there."

"Then you need to go in the normal way. Like a human would." At my blank look, she leaned closer. "You need to be dead."

"Wait, what?"

"Here's the situation—there are several entrances to Hades. I used my dragon sense to get there, which meant I went in a weird way. But if you sneak in through a back way as a living person like I did, the gods are going to notice. Hades or Persephone, maybe even Hecate."

"That's who we're going to find."

"Hecate?" She winced. "Yeah, you're going to want to sneak up on her, from what I've heard."

"That's what I thought."

"Okay, well, you don't want the gods to know you're there. Even if you are the Greek Dragon God. Maybe they wouldn't have a problem with it, but maybe they would. It's not a place for the living, and you would upset the natural balance."

"Okay, so we need to find an entrance that leads us to the River Styx. We'll pretend to be dead people—magically somehow, since I don't want to die quite yet—and we'll sneak in that way."

"Yes. You'll go through all the steps a human soul would go through, ending in judgement and your assignment to your afterlife realm. Once you've made it that far, you should have some relative freedom to sneak around and do what you need to do."

"Okay, we can work with that." I looked at Maximus, who nodded.

"Do you know of any entrances that are still open?" Maximus asked.

Nix shook her head. "I don't know exactly how you should get to the River Styx. Tartarus is the only part of Hades that is actually underground, so you don't want to enter that way."

"The rest isn't underground?" I frowned.

"No. Human interpretation puts them underground because the entrances are generally through caves and in lakes. They're portals that make it look like you're going underground. But in reality, they're taking you to Annatlia, the magical realm of the Greek gods. It's located roughly in southern Greece."

"But what about Mount Olympus? Does only Zeus rule there?" I asked.

She nodded. "Exactly."

Okay, this was starting to make sense. I'd learned a bit about the Greek gods and their realms, but it had been only what I'd managed to read in the last few weeks. Though I'd spoken to a couple of the gods, they hadn't explained all this to me.

"If we're going to cross the River Styx with Charon, we need ancient Greek coins to pay him," Maximus said. "I could conjure replicas, but they wouldn't have the patina of age, so I'm not sure they'd work."

"Where the heck will we get those?" I asked.

"I have a contact at the Museum of Magical History in Magic's Bend," Nix said. "If I explain what it's for, he may let you have two."

"Oh, thank fates." I really didn't want to go robbing any ancient sites to get the coins I needed. Not that I'd know how to find one anyway. "So the next thing we need is a potion that can make us appear to be dead so we don't set off the alarm when we enter."

Jude nodded. "I think Hedy can help with that."

49

A little thrill of excitement surged through me. This sounded like a very cool potion, and I wanted to watch Hedy make it.

"I've found something!" Florian's voice echoed from the back of the stacks.

I turned to see him hurrying out with a large book in his hand. He rushed to the table and set it down, pointing to an old pen and ink illustration. "There. You need to go through the bottomless Alcyonian Lake at Lerna. *That's* how you'll get into Hades."

"Well done," Jude said.

Florian beamed.

I looked at Maximus. "Looks like we're going to hell."

After Nix explained a bit more about Hades and what to expect, she headed to Magic's Bend to try to get us a couple of ancient Greek coins.

I went to my apartment to take the fastest shower in the history of time. All clean, I hopped out and scrubbed myself dry, then hurried into the bedroom. I leaned over the spiral stairs that led down to the living room and shouted to Maximus, "Your turn!"

His footsteps were silent on the stairs up, but he appeared quickly. I tugged my towel closer around me, heating under his quick but appreciative gaze.

"That way." I pointed to the little bathroom.

"When I'm done, I'll get the scuba equipment we need to get to the bottom of the lake and meet you at Hedy's workshop."

"It's a date."

"I wish." His gaze didn't travel any lower over my barely clothed form, but it did heat.

I blushed and turned away, waving my hand. "Go on. We need to get a move on."

While he showered, I tugged on clean clothes. It was now nearly midnight, and we were about to start off on another long adventure. Hopefully Hedy would have a pep-up potion of some kind.

I strapped my fully loaded potions belt around my waist, then grabbed a slim backpack that I loaded full of potion bombs. As I hurried down the stairs and into the living room, I looked over at the kitchen.

Romeo, Poppy, and Eloise sat on the counter. A normal person might think it was gross to have animals on their kitchen counter, but I never cooked in there. Every square inch that wasn't covered by the Menacing Menagerie was littered with potions equipment.

Going somewhere good? Romeo asked.

"Hell."

Ohhhh.

Eloise's eyes brightened.

"Lots of fights in hell, Eloise." I grinned at her, knowing the badger's love for a good battle.

She nodded, excited.

We'll be there if you need us.

Poppy nodded as if she agreed with Romeo, the little flower bobbing on her head. The possum always wore a flower behind her ear, and today, it was a tiny pink rose.

"Thanks, guys."

I left them to do whatever the heck it was they were doing and hurried down the hall and through the castle. I'd been here less than a year, and I still couldn't believe it was my home. The huge, ancient structure was as comforting as it was magical, and I loved it.

The night was dark and crisp as I stepped out onto the main

lawn and headed for Hedy's workshop at the edge. The round tower sat off on its own, just in case one of Hedy's experiments went wrong.

And by wrong, I meant *boom*.

Golden light glittered in the windows, and smoke billowed from the chimney. I knocked on the heavy wooden door, drawing in the scent of roses that bloomed there even in the winter. Some kind of magic of Hedy's, I was sure.

"Come in!" Her voice echoed through the door.

I pushed it open, stepping into a potion-maker's wonderland. The round space was cluttered with tables, which were covered with hundreds of bottles of ingredients and dozens of little tools and bowls. A cauldron bubbled over the hearth, spewing out a glittery white smoke that smelled of lavender and honey. Three miniature cauldrons sat on a table on the left side of the room, each emitting a colorful smoke. Drying herbs hung from the rafters, hundreds of types.

I grinned at Hedy, who wore a flowy dress made of spangly silver fabric. Her lavender hair hung loose down her back, full of tangles and herbs. Normally, it was smooth and shiny.

She turned, revealing that she, too, was carrying an impressive set of luggage beneath her eyes.

"Tired?" I asked.

"Always, these days." She shook her head. "But it's fine. Until we've stopped the Stryx, it's worth it."

I nodded and stepped toward her. "What can I do to help?"

"Here." Hedy handed me a silver spoon that sparked with imbued magic. "You can stir. And be careful to go at a three-quarters speed with a fluttering wrist flick."

I nodded. "Got it."

No matter how good I became with my magic, I'd always love potions. Mastering potions had given me confidence and strength when I'd needed it most, and I'd be forever grateful.

Hedy and I worked together in silence, making something called the draught of living death. By the time it was done, my wrist was sore but my heart was full.

Hedy poured the potion into two little glass vials and handed them to me. The rest of the potion went into a third vial that she set on the table. "That should do it. Drink it right before you enter Hades. You'll still be alive, but it will appear to others as if you are just a soul. Don't let anyone touch you, though. It's just an illusion. You won't actually be as transparent and incorporeal as you look."

I took the vials. "Fantastic, thanks."

"It will only last about twelve hours, so be quick."

"We will."

She reached into her pocket and pulled out a small black stone, then pressed it into my palm. "That is a *very* rare transport charm that will get you out of Hades when you're done with your mission. One of a kind and hard as hell to make. Use it only if you need it."

"Thank you." I stuck it in the pocket of my jeans, which were so tight that the stone wouldn't go anywhere without my permission.

"Oh, and here." She turned and picked up two more vials. "Magical caffeine. Given that it's after midnight and you have a full day's work ahead of you, I think you need it."

"I do. Thank you."

"Use it wisely," she said. "You can't take too much. It'll send your system into overdrive. So this is pretty much it."

"Okay." Now was as good a time as any.

Hedy and I left her workshop. As soon as we stepped out onto the lawn, I spotted Maximus and Nix. They approached from the castle. Maximus was carrying a big bag over one shoulder and a strange, torpedo-like thing in the other hand.

The little machine was roughly four feet long and had a propeller at one end. *Cool.*

Nix raised her hand in the air. "Got your coins!"

They stopped in front of me, and she handed me a heavy gold coin.

I studied it, impressed by the age and importance of it. I looked up at her. "Are you sure the museum doesn't mind?"

"They don't make a habit of handing out artifacts, but considering that the original purpose of this coin was to be given to Charon to cross into Hades, they are making an exception."

"And it will possibly save the world," Maximus added.

Nix grinned. "That too. Both compelling reasons."

"Well, then." I looked at Maximus. "Ready to get dead?"

CHAPTER SIX

Because we were trying to save on transport charms, the friendly transport mage named Emily took us to Lerna, a region in Greece famous for its swamps.

As soon as we arrived, the scent of wet vegetation hit me. The moon shined brightly on Lake Alcyonian in front of us.

I looked at Emily. "Thanks."

She smiled, her dark hair gleaming in the light. "No problem. Be safe."

"You too."

She disappeared back to the Protectorate, and I turned to Maximus, who was setting the bag on the ground, along with the small torpedo-shaped thing that was apparently an underwater scooter that would help us get to the bottom of the lake.

"One thing I should mention about this lake...." I said.

"The Hydra."

"Yep." This was where Heracles had come to fight the famous Lernaean Hydra. "But Heracles killed it. So hopefully there aren't any more."

Maximus studied the calm surface of the lake, his gaze intense. "It's said that the lake is bottomless and that anyone who attempts to cross it will be sucked down." He shrugged. "Good news for us, since that's the direction we're headed."

I patted the underwater scooter. "Maybe we won't even need this thing."

"It'll be useful." Maximus picked it up like it weighed nothing, though it had to be at least fifty pounds. It was about four feet long, with a propeller on one end and handles for us to hang on to. "I like to control my own destiny."

After years as a warrior slave, I couldn't blame him.

I patted the coin that was shoved into my jeans' pocket. Then I pulled the two vials from my other pocket and handed one to Maximus. "Ready?"

He nodded and took the vial, then uncorked it quickly. We both drank the potion. I shuddered at the taste of dust as magic sparked down my limbs.

Maximus's skin began to turn pale. So pale that it became transparent, and he looked like a shadow of himself. I reached out, surprised when my hand didn't drift right through his chest. Hedy had told me we wouldn't be incorporeal, but damned if he didn't look like a ghost.

"Do I look weird, too?" I asked.

"Like a ghost."

"Perfect." I held out my hand for the scuba equipment we'd brought.

Maximus bent to the bag at his feet and removed one of the small tanks that was hooked up to a shoulder harness with a clip at the front. I strapped it on so the tank sat on my back and the straps buckled in front of me. It was far more minimalist than the scuba equipment I'd seen on TV. I picked up the mouthpiece and took an experimental breath. The air was cold and metallic, but it did the job.

"Remember," Maximus said. "Don't hold your breath."

"Or my lungs will explode. Yeah, yeah."

"Not exactly, but close enough."

"I didn't realize you liked scuba diving."

He shrugged. "For most of my life, I never dreamed a person would actually get into the ocean and submerge willingly. Almost no one could even swim back then." He bent again and pulled a mask out of the bag, then handed it to me.

I put it on, feeling like a total nerd.

Maximus put on his equipment quickly and efficiently, seeming comfortable. "This kit is so small we'll only have about fifteen minutes' worth of air. A lot less if we end up very deep."

I nodded.

"If your ears start to bother you from the pressure, squeeze your nose, then blow. It'll help."

"Got it." Now I just wanted to get this over with. I waded into the water, shuddering at the cold. Even though it was a famous beach destination, Greece was chilly in the winter.

Maximus followed, carrying the scooter. As soon as we were up to our chins, he stuck the thing into the water and turned it on. A light attached to the front flared to life, shining a bright beam through the dark water.

Oh, fates. This is insane.

I might be able to control water, but this felt crazy. I sucked in a deep breath, then grabbed onto the handles on the scooter and submerged my head. Maximus did the same, turning a switch so the scooter shot forward. It dragged us through the cold, dark water.

We descended quickly, the water rushing by us.

My heart pounded as we went deeper into the darkness. The white beam of light revealed nothing but endless black water.

Soon, my ears began to ache from the depth, and I reached up with one hand to equalize in the way Maximus had shown me. I nearly lost my grip on the torpedo, and Maximus grabbed me tight.

"Thanks," I tried to say, but it just came out as bubbles.

I gripped the scooter with both hands and hung on tight, my skin cold and heart pounding. Deeper and deeper we went. The water seemed endless, a flooded tunnel right into the earth.

When something flashed in front of our scooter, I gasped. The light had illuminated six large eyes, but most of the detail had been obscured. Fear iced my blood.

Hydra.

I looked around, frantic, but the water was dark on all sides. I shook my hand, igniting the magic in my light stone ring. It flared to life, shedding a bit of light to my left.

The eyes flashed again, along with three snakelike heads.

"Hydra!" I screamed, but the words were only unintelligible bubbles through my mouthpiece.

Maximus saw, though, because he turned toward it.

The creature struck toward us, three massive heads shooting out of the darkness. I cringed away, barely avoiding the beast as Maximus swung back with one arm and punched one of the heads.

He hit the creature so hard that it plowed backward through the water, away from us.

Holy fates, Maximus was strong. Moving any body part underwater was slow and laborious. The water dragged so hard at all of my limbs. But not for Maximus. There was nothing he couldn't do with his gladiator strength.

My heart pounded in my ears as I searched our surroundings, waiting for the beast to come back. As Maximus steered the scooter deeper and deeper into the lake, I drew my sword from the ether. I couldn't behead the thing or it'd grow two heads in place of the one, but there were no rules against stabbing it.

Please let us be nearly there.

When the Hydra flashed in front of our light, I flinched, then tightened my grip on the scooter. It appeared again, to the left, barely illuminated in the glow of my light stone ring.

I raised my sword, the current dragging at my arm. Damn, this was hard.

The Hydra struck, and I didn't flinch. Instead, I thrust out my sword straight toward it and nailed it in the neck. A plume of green blood burst from the Hydra as it jerked backward, darting away.

No way I was lucky enough to have driven it off with just one blow.

When the water in front of us turned an even murkier black in the light of the scooter, relief flooded me. We had to be close.

The Hydra darted toward us again, this time from the right. Maximus delivered a fierce punch to the creature's left head right before the portal to Hades sucked us in.

The creature's angry eyes were the last thing I saw before the ether dragged me toward hell.

When it spat me out on a grassy field, I yanked the mouthpiece away and gasped. I lay flat on my back, staring up at a starless sky. Next to me, Maximus was sprawled out.

He removed the mouthpiece and turned to me. "You okay?"

I yanked off my mask and nodded. "Fine."

I was wet and cold and miserable.

Except, not totally miserable. Actually, it felt good to be here.

Oh, crap. Did I like hell?

I did *not* want to like hell.

I shook away the thought, and I drew in a breath, then commanded the water that soaked my clothes to evaporate. It took a moment, but finally, it worked. I was dry. Mostly.

I did the same for Maximus, and he grinned, pulling me close to press a kiss to his forehead. "Thanks."

Despite the fact that he was still ghostly and so was I, I could feel the warmth of his kiss. I leaned into it briefly, but it was over in the blink of an eye.

"Anytime." Quickly, I tugged off the scuba tank and inspected our surroundings. We were on a flat plain covered in scrubby black grass. It grew three feet tall, but we lay in a flattened patch.

"Let's hide this equipment," Maximus said.

I helped him stash the mask, tanks, and scooter in the grass, then stood and brushed off my hands. The night was silent around us, without even the sound of animals rustling in the brush. I'd grown used to hearing them when I was outside, and their absence was telling.

Nothing wanted to be here.

Maximus spun in a circle, inspecting our surroundings. "It all looks the same."

It did, unfortunately. Nothing but endless fields, each view indistinguishable from the next. But I could make out the sound of water in the distance, just ahead of us. I could sense it, too, with the gift from Poseidon.

I pointed. "I hear the river that way."

"Ready?"

I nodded and set off, pushing through the tall grass. It scraped at my hands, surprisingly sharp for something so slender and delicate. I raised my hands above the grass, avoiding the sting.

We neared the River Styx, and the air seemed to grow heavier. Darker. As if misery were a room fragrance and someone had gone nuts with the spray bottle. I breathed shallowly through my mouth, trying not to draw it too deeply into me.

When I spotted the river, I gasped. It was almost a hundred yards wide.

"It's huge," I murmured.

"Where's the boatman?"

I turned to look up and down the river, but he was nowhere to be seen. There wasn't a bit of movement on the river, actually.

"I don't think he gets a lot of business, these days. Not a lot of people believe in the Greek gods. At least, not as their primary form of religion."

"If this is where they'd end up in the afterlife, I can't say that I blame them."

"No, it sucks." I squinted down the river, spotting a lump along the shore. It looked like it was shaped roughly like a boat. "I see something down there."

We hurried down the shore toward the lump. It was definitely a boat. Long and broad with an open cargo space. Like a huge wooden dingy, really. As we neared, it moved. A figure stood up.

"Charon," I murmured. He must have been napping. Not what I expected from the infernal ferryman, but what did I know?

"Who goes there?" His voice rumbled like the fires of hell. He turned, his eyes glowing bright red from beneath his dark hood.

"We've..." Ah, what exactly? "Died."

"We need to go to the other side," Maximus said.

We approached to stand right in front of the boat, so close that I could smell the brimstone of Charon's breath. It was impossible to see what he really looked like beneath the flowing black cloak, but his flaming eyes were enough of a hint that I probably didn't want too much detail.

"It's been over three hundred years since someone has arrived on these shores seeking passage." His voice sounded rusty from disuse, and I wondered if he'd been sleeping since then.

I swallowed the jokes I wanted to make and dug into my

pocket, then held out the coin in my palm. "We brought payment."

Charon's eyes traveled between the two of us. "Both of you?"

Maximus pulled out his coin. "Both."

Charon continued to stare at us, gaze suspicious.

I resisted shifting on my feet. Instead, I tried to look miserable about being dead. Tension raised the hair on my arms as Charon kept staring.

Finally, he swept his arm to the side in a pseudo-welcoming gesture. "You may board."

I sucked in a deep breath and boarded the ship of the dead. It rocked gently beneath my feet, and some of the hope in my body seemed to leak out through the soles of my feet. Though I wasn't really dead and headed to a lifetime of damnation, my soul didn't seem to know that.

In fairness, all souls probably hated crossing the Styx. It was probably why Charon was nothing but a shriveled husk with fiery eyes.

Charon held out his hand, and I was satisfied to note that I'd been right. Shriveled husk. Then I felt a bit bad for him. Poor guy.

"Well?" he snapped.

"Sorry." I shoved the coin into his hand.

Maximus handed his over more gracefully.

"Sit down and stay quiet, miserable mortals." Loathing coated his voice, and I felt a bit less bad for him.

Maximus and I sat at the back of the boat on one of the benches that lined the sides. Charon bent and picked up a long pole that had been sitting in the bottom of the vessel, then moved to the front. He stuck the pole in the water and began to punt us across the river.

I glanced at Maximus, whose face was drawn tight. I had a feeling mine looked the same.

All around, the river rushed quietly by us. It swirled, dark and deep, and I swore I could see figures in it. Souls?

I shivered and looked away. It felt like my chest was filling up with darkness as we made our way slowly across the river. The closer we got to the other side, the worse it felt.

An icy hand gripped my forearm, and I nearly shrieked. I bit it back and glanced down, heart in my throat.

A skeletal, ghostly hand had reached up from the water and grabbed me. I reached for it, trying to pry it off, and leaned over the side of the boat to look into the black eyes of one of the damned. The figure stared up at me, hatred and evil glowing in its coal dark eyes.

Oh, this was definitely one of the damned. And he'd been damned for good reason.

"You are filled with darkness." Charon cackled "They like you."

I shifted, not liking the sound of that.

"Well, I don't like them." I grabbed the hand and yanked, but it held firm. Anger and fear burst in my chest like bubbles full of black tar.

Maximus reached over and grabbed the hand, prying it off with his gladiator strength. He flung the creature back into the water. It splashed, hissing angrily.

"Thanks." I looked into the water, my heart thudding. I didn't want to attract these damned monsters. There was darkness inside me, but I didn't want it. Didn't like it. It wasn't *me*.

And I didn't want to feel so comfortable in this place. I was afraid of the souls, but not of this place, which was weird. Weird and horrible.

The water rippled, and anxiety crept along my back. When the creature lunged out of the water, reaching for me, I bit back another scream and dodged away. It was too fast, though, grasping for my arm. Maximus grabbed it, prying it off, but before he'd even flung it away, another grabbed for me. And another.

Two came out of the water simultaneously, reaching for my arms.

Panic flared, bringing cold fear with it.

"No!" The word exploded out of me, and I called upon all the goodness within my heart. Anything that was light and kind, I dragged it to the surface, imagining that it was a bright white light.

The creatures of the damned fell back from me, their eyes flashing with hatred. They slipped into the water.

"Good." I turned back to find Charon staring at me, red gaze assessing.

Damn.

I shrank into myself, trying to look non-threatening. Normal.

"I wonder what the judges will think of you," he mused.

Frankly, I didn't care. The Greek gods had given me their powers, but I wasn't interested in their judgement of me. I'd read a lot of the myths, and frankly, I wasn't impressed with them. Between all the trickery and cruelty and misogyny, a lot of the gods were jerks.

It was my job to be the Greek Dragon God—to use their magic to make the world a better place. But I didn't care what they thought of me.

The rest of the journey continued in silence. I couldn't help but glance anxiously at the water as we crossed. Several times, I met the hateful gaze of one of the damned, floating just below the surface, but they only stared. Maximus sat at my side, ready to defend me. But more importantly, I was ready to defend myself. Those bastards didn't stand a chance.

By the time we reached the other side, I was vibrating with tension.

The boat drifted to a stop alongside the bank, and Charon gestured with his arm. "Get out."

I climbed out of the boat, swallowing a sarcastic thank you, and looked at Maximus.

He nodded, and we headed away from the boat. I could feel Charon's burning gaze on my back, and I hoped the rest of the denizens of Hades weren't as suspicious of us.

We climbed the river bank quickly. As soon as we reached the top, I spotted the gates of hell. They were made of massive pieces of black wrought iron that twisted and turned, rising high toward the black sky. Had to be the work of Hephaestus. A massive black mound lay before them.

Then it moved.

I blinked.

Slowly, a huge creature rose to its feet. It had inky black fur and four huge paws. Three heads.

Cerberus.

The three-headed dog turned to us, blinking six yellow eyes. Three mouths fell open, revealing fangs as long as my legs. A growl rose in the beast's chest.

I swallowed hard and stepped closer to Maximus.

"We must approach," he said.

I nodded, continuing forward on shaky legs. I liked animals. All of them, even the mean ones. I didn't love it if they were mean *to* me. But in general, I thought they were fine. They were just doing their animal jobs, being murderous crocodiles and the like.

Except it was Cerberus's job to inspect *us*.

So that made this a bit more complicated.

We walked toward the dog. With every step, I shook harder, unable to keep my eyes away from the monster's many sharp teeth. It had breath like dead bodies and claws that could tear open my ribs with one flick.

"Nice doggie," I murmured.

Cerberus looked at me like I was an idiot.

I probably was.

He leaned low to sniff us, warm air puffing out of his three nostrils. My heart thundered and my skin chilled.

He stopped, holding dead still. A growl rose in his chest, louder and fiercer than the one before. He sniffed again.

Growled again.

Oh, fates.

Cerberus could smell that we were still living, and he knew that something was *definitely* wrong.

CHAPTER SEVEN

Shit. Shit. Shit.

The giant hellhound was about to bite our heads off because he knew we were breaking in.

Frantically, my mind raced. How the hell were we going to get out of this?

He's just an animal.

Big, mean, and strong. But an animal like any other.

I sucked in a deep breath and called on the magic that Artemis had given me. If I could just get inside his head....

I tried to replicate what had happened with the wolf, forcing my life force inside Cerberus's body. He growled and puffed above us, leaning lower as if to take a bite. My heart thundered and sweat rolled down my back.

Then it worked. My consciousness melded with Cerberus's. I could see myself and Maximus standing in front of me. So tiny.

And I could feel Cerberus's confusion. We didn't smell right. Were we bad?

No.

I tried to convince the dog, working like a spy implanted within his own mind. He shook his heads, clearly confused.

At my feet, Maximus looked equally confused by Cerberus's change in demeanor. Then he looked at my body, and understanding dawned.

It took a while, but I felt the great dog calming. I tried to feed him soothing energy, melding my own consciousness with his. He settled down, leaning back on his haunches and tilting his heads to look at us.

Okay, okay. This wasn't so bad. He probably wasn't going to eat us.

Lie down. Take a nap. You're a good boy.

I could feel his pleasure, and he did as I asked, settling down into his previous mountain-like form. He sighed, a big billowy huff, then closed his eyes.

I returned to my body.

"You did that?" Maximus whispered.

I nodded. "Let's go in."

We crept around Cerberus, who sighed in his sleep, sending puffs of horrible dead-body breath wafting over us. I held my breath, trying not to gag.

As we stepped beneath the massive iron gates that led into the depth of Hades, I shivered. The air here was even more horrible feeling, and a thick fog obscured our vision. It felt like tiny stinging gnats flew through the air, biting and nipping.

"How did you do that?" Maximus asked as we walked slowly through the fog. "With a hellhound that big? It didn't make it harder?"

"No. My gift from Artemis is really turning out to be my favorite. And it wasn't hard. He's just a dog. I mean, he's got some powerful weapons, but at the end of the day, he just wants to be told he's a good boy."

Maximus grinned.

The fog cleared ahead of us, revealing a long road that cut through a barren field. Mist hovered over grass, and the road was paved with large flat rocks that fit together perfectly. The path itself looked endless. I swallowed hard, any positive memories of Cerberus fading.

Maximus reached for my hand, and despite our ghostly appearances, I could feel his warmth. I clung to it, drawing in a steady breath and stepping onto the road.

On either side of the path, the mist coalesced to form shadowy figures. Four of them. They appeared to be wearing long, hooded cloaks, a lot like the boatman had worn. Cold magic rolled out from their forms, a wintry breeze that froze my skin. They drifted onto the road, floating toward us.

"They must be escorts," I murmured to Maximus.

As they neared, the air grew even colder. My teeth began to chatter and my limbs shook. It took everything I had to stiffen my spine and stare straight at the ghostly figures. This place made me intensely uncomfortable, but I wouldn't let it beat me.

They didn't speak as they surrounded us. Two stood next to me and two next to Maximus. Then they began to walk.

Instinct propelled me forward, and Maximus did the same. Silently, we walked down the path as the mist rolled alongside us. Our guards were silent, but it was clear they wouldn't let us move about unescorted. They stuck so close that I could almost feel the cold mist of their cloaks brushing against my arm.

We walked for a while—how long, I couldn't tell—until finally, we crested a hill. In the distance, I spotted a massive temple. Unlike most Greek temples, it was painted entirely black. The tall columns were enormous, supporting a roof that had to be a hundred yards across. Behind the building, lightning struck.

The shadowy guards continued down the hill, heading toward the fortress.

I swallowed hard, and followed.

"We'll be judged there," I whispered to Maximus, remembering what Nix had said.

"Let the tricky part begin."

He was right. It would be tricky. From what I knew of Hades, we would stand before three judges—Rhadamanthus, Minos, and Aeacus. They would determine which region of Hades we would end up in, and from there, we could sneak away and find Hecate. If we were lucky, we'd end up in the same region and be able to start our hunt in secret. If we didn't, we'd have to escape the guards while being transported to our region and start to hunt for Hecate. Problem with that plan was that they might sound an alarm for escaped souls.

I crossed my fingers that I'd end up in the same place as Maximus.

It was unlikely that we'd go to Tartarus. Neither of us was a complete bastard. And since neither of us—to my knowledge—was suffering from a deep and unrequited love, we wouldn't end up in the Mourning Fields, either. Which was good, because it sounded almost worse than Tartarus. Elysium was unlikely, at least for me. That was reserved for true heroes. So odds were best that I'd go to the Asphodel Meadows, where most souls went after death. The people there were just normal people—kinda good and kinda bad. No super jerks or superheroes. I had money on Maximus going to Elysium, and if that were the case, we'd deal with it when the time came.

I shook away thoughts of what was to come and focused on the lay of the land as we approached the temple. It was flat all around, with nothing to see in the distance besides the massive temple ahead of us. The air smelled vaguely stale, as if we were in an old closet. But then, we were the first souls in hundreds of years, according to Charon.

We reached the massive temple and began to ascend the stairs. There were thirteen of them, and I counted each to keep my mind under control. I hated this place—hated that it was the home of Hades, the one who had given me the death power I found to be so dreadfully useful. Hated that I felt comfortable here, despite the terror that surrounded me.

Two massive black wooden doors swung open as we neared, and the guards stepped back, gesturing for us to walk through.

I did, keeping my eyes straight ahead and my spine stiff. Maximus was beside me, which frankly, made most things better.

We entered a massive room where the ceiling soared fifty feet high. The marble floor was shiny and smooth beneath my feet, the black stone glinting in the light of a hundred glass lamps. The air sparked with energy, and I shivered.

Life seemed to fill the air here, despite its emptiness. It was almost as if I could feel the souls of those who had passed through on their way to judgement.

The doors slammed shut behind us, and I turned. They were shut tight, all hope of escape long gone. I looked at Maximus.

"Not very welcoming, is it?" he asked.

"Nope." I started toward the doors on the far side of the hall. I had no idea where we were supposed to go, but I didn't want to wait around. Not just because we were tight on time, but because standing here made my skin crawl.

Maximus joined me, and we strode forward, our steps matched. As we neared the second set of doors, they swung open. Maximus stopped abruptly, and instinct made me follow suit. The air within the chamber was repellent.

Decisions were made in that room. Big ones. The kind that determined where you'd spend eternity, which was about the biggest decision I could imagine. I waited, heart pounding, for what felt like a decade. The air fizzed with the energy of departed souls, making me shift uncomfortably on my feet.

"Enter." The voice boomed through the door, and I barely resisted jumping.

I glanced at Maximus. He hiked a shoulder and nodded.

I sucked in a deep breath and followed him through the doors.

The room within was smaller, but not by much. There was a long table in front of us. Three men sat at it, each looking like one of those big white statues of old bearded men wearing robes.

Quintessential ancient Greek Smart Guy. No question.

They were so similar that it was hard to tell them apart.

"You are here to be judged," said the one in the middle. His voice echoed through the room, and his long beard quivered as he spoke. "I am Rhadamanthus."

The one to his left inclined his head. "I am Minos."

The one to his right copied the gesture. "I am Aeacus."

"We are the three judges," Rhadamanthus said. "And we will determine the destination of your soul."

I stayed quiet, and Maximus did the same. Since I didn't know what was proper protocol here, better to play it silent and afraid. That seemed like a normal attitude for the dead.

"Step forward, Maximus Valerius," Rhadamanthus intoned.

I twitched, startled that they knew his name. Did that mean they would recognize me as the Greek Dragon God? Or would they not care? Were they even gods? There were so many small ones I couldn't remember them all. If they weren't gods, they'd have no reason to know about the Greek Dragon Gods.

Maximus stepped forward, and I watched him, my eyes glued to his broad shoulders. The three judges leaned forward, staring hard at him. Their eyes burned with an eerie yellow fire, magic sparking within their depths.

Seconds ticked by, and I barely resisted shifting uncomfortably as I waited. When Rhadamanthus finally nodded, my shoulders tightened.

"You have accomplished great deeds on earth," he said. "Heroic deeds."

I almost grinned, glad that the judges could see how good Maximus was.

"You will go to Elysium."

My smile fell.

Shit.

The hero's realm. No way I would qualify for that.

I'd kind of expected him to go there, but now we'd need to sort out a way to escape unnoticed while they were escorting us to our final destinations.

"Step aside," Rhadamanthus said.

Maximus did as he was told, and the judges called me forward. I stepped up to them, my cheeks heating. Their gazes burned into me as I stood before them, and I swore I could feel them inside my chest. Everything within me was on fire, and it was as if they were looking into my organs. Into my heart and soul. What they'd see in there, I had no idea.

If I hadn't been frozen solid, I'd have shifted nervously. As it was, I couldn't move an inch.

"Hmmmm," Rhadamanthus said. "You never completed your potential."

Maybe because I'm not really dead yet.

But I kept my mouth shut.

My shoulders tightened as I waited. This was it. He was going to send me to the Asphodel Meadows, and we'd have to jumpstart our plan and break away before we found a quiet place to sneak off.

"However, the extent of your good deeds is great." He nodded. "You will go to Elysium as well."

My brows jumped, and I almost asked, "Really?"

73

Fortunately, my jaw was still frozen solid with nerves. They'd take a while to fade. I might be comfortable in Hades, but that didn't mean I was comfortable with everyone in it. And I didn't like these judges.

I just nodded and moved toward Maximus.

This was good. This was very good. Not the place I'd expected to end up, but we'd be together.

There was a small smile on Maximus's face, as if he'd expected me to end up in the hero's realm. He was alone in that expectation, but I appreciated it.

I could feel the eyes of the judges as I stopped next to Maximus. Four shadowy figures drifted out of the wall. More escorts.

We followed them from the room, and never once did the burn of the judges' gazes disappear. The guards led us through a wide hallway, past an enormous room decorated in black marble and gold. Within the room, a man sat on a throne of ebony. He was twice the size of a normal person, with flowing black hair and blazing blue eyes. A tall golden scepter was clutched in his hand.

His eyes fell upon me briefly as I walked in front of his open door, and a shiver of awareness raced over me.

Hades.

It had to be Hades.

Had he recognized me? He should. I had his magic.

But I appeared to be dead.

My heart thundered in my ears as I waited for a shout to sound from behind us. He would call out and stop us. Of course he would. We were intruders.

But there was only silence.

Either he thought I was shit at my Dragon God job and had died, or he was going to let me try to complete my task here. The gods were famous for their fickle natures. They'd give their power one minute and ignore you the next.

Maybe he was just letting me get on with it.

I sure hoped that was the case.

The guards led us to a huge round room. Four wide doors exited the space—not including the one we'd entered from—and the guards turned to the one that was made of white marble. It was the only thing white that I'd seen in all of Hades, and it gleamed so brightly it almost blinded me. Another door was made of thick black iron, another of pale wood, and the last of pink quartz.

The white door disappeared as we neared, and the guards stepped to the side, gesturing for us to go through.

Maximus and I strode through without glancing back. As soon as we crossed the threshold, the air changed. It smelled fresher. Almost like spring grass.

The sun beat down brightly on a rolling green field. In the distance, a small city sat on a hill. White buildings filled the city, and there would be people there. Or souls, at least.

I turned back to the door to find it gone.

My shoulders relaxed for the first time since we'd arrived in hell.

"We made it," I said.

"In Elysium, no less."

"Apparently we're heroes."

"Because of what you're doing," Maximus said. "Trying to fight the Stryx."

I warmed at his words. "Well, whatever the case, let's find our way to Hecate."

"As expected, we're not being guarded. But we should find someone to ask."

"Agreed." I started toward the city, my steps quick. I had no idea how to find Hecate, but at least we now had freedom of movement and there were no angry gods peeved by the fact that we'd broken in. If Hades realized the truth, he was ignoring it.

The city was quiet as we approached, though the buildings looked lived in. Plants and vases sat in the windows of the houses, and smoke drifted up from chimneys. They were simple white structures, very classical Greece. The smell of food wafted on the air.

But there was no noise. It was so quiet that I'd have heard a bird sing. Except there were no birds either.

"Where is everyone?" I asked.

"Some sources report that the Greek Underworld is full of shades. They're people—and they look like they used to on earth—but they don't live full lives like humans do. They sort of drift through, doing the things they did on earth, but they aren't fully present."

I'd read something like that and hated the sound of it. I shivered and stepped onto the road that led into town. Maximus and I walked quickly down the street between the white houses, searching for a sign of anyone.

Twice, I thought I saw figures drift past windows inside the houses, but they were gone quickly.

When we arrived at the town square, I finally saw a bunch of people. They were transparent, like Maximus and me, but otherwise, they looked normal. There were at least twenty of them, all gathered around various pursuits. There was a massive fountain in the middle of the square, and people stood next to it, staring at the water. Children played a game with a hoop and a stick, while two old men played a game with little dice. There were even two ghosts dancing, though they didn't look particularly thrilled.

In fact, no one looked thrilled. Not miserable either. Just...existing.

It was a city full of ghosts.

"Which one should we speak to?" Maximus asked.

"How do we speak to them if they are so silent? No one is talking."

"Odysseus sacrificed a lamb, and whichever shade drank the blood could then speak to him."

"Damn. No lamb. And I don't think I have the stomach for that anyway." I looked at him. "But I'm glad you read *The Odyssey*."

He shrugged, a grin tugging at the corner of his mouth. "It's how I learned to read. There was a smuggled copy going around the slave quarters. We didn't have the whole thing—that would have been more than one scroll. But we had the part about the Underworld. It was literally more valuable than gold to us."

It was a poignant image, and I was reminded anew of the hardships Maximus had faced.

"Think they'd drink my blood?" I asked.

Maximus nodded. "I think they'll drink human blood. But they can have mine."

"I don't mind."

"I have a lot more blood."

"You *need* a lot more blood to run that big body of yours."

He sighed and chuckled at the same time. "Consider this like a...chivalric gesture. I can't open the car door or bring you flowers since we have no time for dates, so I'll donate blood to the dead shades so they'll tell us the secrets of the Underworld."

I laughed low in my throat. "How romantic."

"Hard to resist, isn't it?"

I grinned widely. "Very."

"Good. Glad you agree."

"I'll cut you a deal. You donate to the first shade, and if that doesn't work, I'll donate to the second."

"Like going Dutch on the check?"

"Sure."

"Fair enough." He spun in a circle, then pointed. "That one looks promising."

I turned to took, spotting an old man sitting under a tree. He looked peaceful and about as old as the sun, with a long beard and a severely wrinkled face. "He does look good."

Old people always knew the most stuff.

We set off across the square, walking at a sedate pace. I didn't know what the shades would do if we revealed ourselves to be not quite dead, but I didn't want to find out.

We stopped in front of the old man, who blinked and looked up at us.

"Hi," I said. "Can you speak to us?"

He frowned, clearly confused.

"Looks like a no." Maximus's magic swelled on the air, bringing with it the light scent of cedar. A small blade and bowl appeared in his hands, and he quickly made a cut on his forearm, letting the blood pour into the little bowl.

"If he doesn't want the blood, he's going to think you're really freaking weird."

A smile tugged at the corner of his mouth, and he handed the bowl to the man. "A sacrifice."

The man smiled, clearly understanding. Then he drank the blood.

Ew.

If he wasn't a vampire, which he didn't look to be, that was mega gross. But it was bad manners to comment on someone's food, so I snapped my mouth shut.

The man smacked his mouth, his eyes brighter than before. "Thank you."

Maximus nodded.

"I am Aklos. How can I help you?"

"We are looking for Hecate," Maximus said.

"That miserable witch? You'd be better off playing fetch with Cerberus."

I had a feeling that fetch with Cerberus wouldn't end well for us, which meant that Hecate was a *real* piece of work.

"All the same," Maximus said. "We seek her. Do you know how we can find her?"

The old man shrugged. "First, you need to get out of Elysium. You won't find the likes of her in the hero's realm."

"No, I imagine not," Maximus said. "But where is she?"

"In her own realm, situated between Tartarus and the Asphodel Fields. There's an entrance to that realm at the top of that mountain." He pointed toward an extremely creepy-looking black mountain. Lightning flashed overhead, but it was so far away I couldn't hear it. "But you'll need the Keys to the Underworld to get through the gate."

"Where would we get those?" Maximus asked.

The old man's eyes twinkled. "You're in luck. Aeacus holds the Keys to the Underworld, but be aware that there are guards at the gate. Only Aeacus wields the key."

I frowned. "Only Aeacus , or someone who *looks* like Aeacus."

The old man shrugged. "I'm not sure it matters. There is a guard at the gate who will expect him to be the one wielding it."

"Where can we find Aeacus?" Maximus asked.

The man grinned. "He just so happens to dine several days a week with Rhadamanthus, who rules this realm."

"The judge?" I asked.

The old man's eyes flicked to me. "The very same."

He'd chosen us for his realm. Somehow, that made me feel even better about ending up here.

"Where do they dine?" Maximus asked.

The old man pointed behind us. "Go that way. It won't be long before you see the enormous house at the edge of town.

That is Rhadamanthus's accommodation. They will eat there, if they are indeed meeting tonight."

Fingers crossed.

"Thank you," Maximus said.

The man nodded. "Likewise. But be careful. If the judges catch you trying to steal, you will be sent to Tartarus."

Yikes. I swallowed hard. That could be a problem.

CHAPTER EIGHT

We left Aklos relaxing under the tree and cut back across the square, heading toward the house that he'd mentioned. The sun was dipping down toward the horizon, so hopefully dinner would be soon.

The shades that played and sat within the square paid us no mind, and we hurried past them. We went down a wide street bordered on either side by large, judicial-looking buildings.

When I spotted the enormous house at the end of the road, I grinned. "Twenty bucks that's the judge's place."

"I didn't take him to be a subtle guy, so I won't take that bet."

"Smart move." He'd have lost.

We walked sedately toward the house, cutting down a side street to walk around to the back.

"Do you see a way in?" I asked. There weren't many doors, especially not along the side of the house.

"Not yet." We turned to walk along the back of the house, and I spotted a small door.

A harried-looking shade rushed from the door, an apron tied around her front. She didn't speak, but she didn't have to.

I nodded toward her as she passed. "She looks like cooking staff."

"Kitchen is a good place to do recon. Let's go in."

"I like how you think." I walked toward the door like I knew what I was doing, stepping into a bustling kitchen that smelled of amazing food.

Strangely, though, I wasn't hungry. Maybe it was the potion that made me seem partially dead, but I had no desire to eat. I shivered, wanting to get back to my normal body as quickly as possible.

No one stopped us, but then, this didn't seem like the kind of place where people snuck around doing things they shouldn't. They might not even know what to do with us if they did try to interrogate us.

The judges, however... If they saw us, they'd know. We'd need a way around that.

"Let's see if we can find the dining room," I whispered. "If Aeacus is here, I bet he'll be at the table."

Maximus nodded, and we strode away from the kitchen. Our disguise as a shade worked well, because no one said a word to us.

The massive hallway that we entered was made entirely of white marble. It was cold and clean, and we followed it to a large room set with a big wooden table.

Bingo.

The room was empty, so I searched for a place to hide.

"There." Maximus pointed to a darkened alcove on the wall to our right.

We hurried toward it, slipping into the shadows. There was another door in there, which Maximus tested. It led right outside into a pretty courtyard.

"Perfect." I nodded. "If he arrives, we'll sneak out that way if we need to."

"Let's get comfortable, then."

I sank down against the wall, careful to keep myself in the shadows of the alcove. Maximus joined me, and despite the potion we'd taken to make ourselves look like shades, I could feel the warmth of him.

I leaned against his shoulder, resting my head and eyes for a moment.

"Hell is better with you in it," Maximus said.

"That's because we're in heaven, dummy." Kinda, at least. The ancient Greek version of it. It, too, was comfortable to me, in a weird, distant way.

"With you, any place is heaven."

I stifled a giggle at the ridiculous phrase and looked up at him.

His eyes twinkled with humor. "I know that was over the top, but the sentiment remains."

"Aw, you say the sweetest things."

"You should see how men wooed women in my day. A lot of flowery language and then..."

"Boom, you were chattel for life."

He shrugged lightly. "Not always, but too often. Women didn't have many rights to speak of then."

"You prefer modern day?"

"Most definitely."

I nodded and leaned my head back against his shoulder. "Good."

I didn't want some loser who longed for the day when women were back in the kitchens. That was a good life for many women, but only if they got to choose it. Ancient times weren't great for choice.

Choice.

What an interesting concept.

I hadn't chosen to be a Dragon God. I hadn't chosen the

Greeks as my patrons. But they were what I'd gotten. And that was life—play the cards you were dealt. And they were good cards. I could make a difference with these cards.

But in some things, we got to choose. For me, that meant choosing Maximus. It was becoming clearer with every day. I hadn't known him long, but my instincts were dead-on. And my feelings were starting to become pretty insistent.

If I made it out of this whole thing alive, I'd be choosing Maximus. In whatever capacity he'd have me.

Maximus squeezed my hand, as if he knew what I was thinking. I smiled.

A few minutes later, he nudged my shoulder. "They're arriving."

I leaned out to look, spotting two figures walking into the room.

Rhadamanthus and Aeacus.

Jackpot.

They each took a seat at the long table, one at either end. I inspected Aeacus's apparel, looking for any keys hanging around his neck or stuffed into large pockets. There was just one pocket that I could see, and I hoped the key would be in there.

"That's our cue," I murmured.

Before I could get up, three tiny figures appeared in front of me. The Menacing Menagerie, and they looked like ghosts.

"What are you doing here?" I hissed.

Helping. Romeo the raccoon grinned toothily at me.

I looked at Poppy and Eloise, who both grinned. "How are you ghostly?"

Took some potion from the purple-haired witch.

I remembered the third bottle of potion that Hedy had set on the table in her workshop after we'd made the batch. I frowned at Romeo. "Stole, you mean."

No. We didn't steal. The Cats of Catastrophe stole it for us.

"So you teamed up with some famous cat burglars"—who were actually cats—"and stole some valuable potion?"

To help you.

I sighed. "Thanks. But you need to be careful. I don't want you getting stuck here."

He nodded eagerly. Honestly, I was glad to have him on my side. Who knew what kind of help we could need, and these three were pretty clever. It was dangerous, though. Raccoons didn't usually gain admittance to Elysium. If anyone saw him or Eloise or Poppy, they'd know something was up. At least they'd entered this realm while seeming to be dead, so it shouldn't alert the gods. Hopefully it wouldn't be a problem that they hadn't crossed the Styx with Charon.

I glanced at Maximus. "Let's get out of here and come up with a plan."

He nodded, and we slipped out the door into the courtyard. The Menacing Menagerie followed, and we all ducked behind a huge bush. The sun had sunk below the horizon, and the sky was illuminated with a bright pink light.

"How do you want to do this?" Maximus asked.

I looked down at my potion belt and pulled out two tiny vials. I stared at them a moment, debating my options. Then I nodded and looked up at Maximus. "These are invisibility potions." I looked down at Romeo. "If I give you an invisibility potion, do you think you can sneak the key out of that man's pocket? The one who was sitting closest to us?"

Romeo nodded eagerly. *I picked up some pointers from Muffin.*

"Good." I explained the rest of my plan to Maximus, who nodded, then I handed the invisibility potion to Romeo, who grabbed it with his little paw. "Be careful."

He nodded.

"Split it between the three of you and take it now. It should last a while. We don't need anyone seeing you."

He uncorked it and held it out to Eloise and Poppy. Their hands weren't as agile as his, so he helped them drink. One by one, they disappeared. Then he took the last swig and saluted me right before he disappeared.

"I can think of no finer army," Maximus said, a grin in his voice.

I was sure the Menacing Menagerie were eating that up.

"Let's take ours. We'll all be able to see each other since we've taken the same potion. But it won't last long." I uncorked the bottle.

He nodded. "We'll be quick."

I took a half swig of the potion, which was two doses for people our size. The thick taste of mud coated my tongue, and I tried not to gag.

"Ugh, here." I handed it to Maximus.

"Cheers." He took it and swallowed.

Ice shivered down my limbs as the potion went to work. A moment later, I could see the Menacing Menagerie. Then Maximus appeared, the potion clearly working on him as well.

We headed around the building toward the kitchen, moving quickly. We cut through the bustling space again, drawing no looks this time. I saw Romeo give the trash bin one longing glance, but he soldiered on. Once we were in the hall that led to the main dining room, we ducked into a small alcove and waited.

I leaned toward Maximus. "Can you conjure two tiny pairs of scissors?"

He and I both had very weird but specific jobs during this heist. He nodded, his magic flaring so lightly that I wouldn't have sensed it if I hadn't been waiting for it. He handed me a tiny pair of silver scissors, and I gripped them in my hand. He kept the other pair for himself.

When two pairs of footsteps sounded in the hall, we peered around the edge of the alcove.

Two shades, a man and a woman, each carrying a tray with a large bowl on it. Perfect.

I dug into my potion bag, finding a stunner potion bomb. It was one of the weaker ones, and when ingested, it would cause drowsiness. I unscrewed the little metal cap that kept the liquid locked inside, then looked at Maximus. "Distraction?"

"On it." He kept his voice whisper low. Then he whistled, sounding just like a bird.

The servers stopped dead in their tracks, eyes wide. They were clearly not used to birds. They looked at each other, confused, and I darted out from the alcove, tipping my potion bomb over each of their big bowls of soup. My steps were silent enough, and my invisibility potion definitely worked, because they didn't notice me at all.

I was careful to add just a few drops, and when I was done, I ducked back into the alcove.

Breath held, I watched the servers.

The one on the left shrugged. "Strange."

"Very," said the other.

Huh, weird. I could understand ancient Greek. I'd been able to read it before, though, so I supposed it made sense.

They continued on their way, moving sedately down the hall, trays carefully balanced. When they entered the main serving room, we followed, moving quickly and quietly behind them.

The five of us stopped near the wall, waiting for them to serve the soup. I stared, breath held, as the two judges sipped at their spoons. The servers turned and went back to the kitchen, but I gave it a couple more minutes. Hopefully the judges wouldn't go facedown in their dinner. That would definitely alert suspicion.

After a little while, their shoulders sagged, and the hum of their conversation slowed. It was working.

Maximus glanced at me, and I nodded, then gestured to Romeo, Poppy, and Eloise. They sprinted forward on silent feet. Romeo stood on his hind legs, his little arm stretched up toward the loose pocket in the judge's robes.

Please let the key be there.

Romeo was too short, unable to get his hand all the way into the pocket. Eloise scooted under him, her sturdy badger form lifting him up just high enough that he could reach in.

I held my breath as he dug around, hoping the judge couldn't feel him. The man twitched once, but didn't look down. Or worse, move his hand toward his pocket.

When Romeo yanked a big golden key out of the judge's pocket, I wanted to whoop with victory. Which I didn't, obviously, because that would be dumb as hell.

The Menacing Menagerie raced back toward us, and I gestured for them to keep going. We'd meet at the bush where we'd hidden earlier.

With the key safely out of the room, it was time for me and Maximus to get to work.

Silently, we approached the judges. I headed for Aeacus, while he took Rhadamanthus. As I passed by the table, I studied the judges. Their eyelids drooped, and they moved their spoons like they were sloths.

Hmmm. Almost too much potion.

Dang.

I picked up the pace, sneaking behind Aeacus. He had grizzled white hair, and I gagged slightly at what I might have to use it for.

No time for that.

Being grossed out would only slow me down. I ignored it and used the tiny scissors to snip off a bit of hair, which I shoved into my pocket. I looked up to see Maximus finish the same job with Rhadamanthus.

Then we got the heck out of there, hurrying back down the hall and through the kitchens.

It was full dark by the time we made it outside, and the Menacing Menagerie were waiting for us.

I crouched behind the bushes and rubbed Romeo's head. "Well done, guys."

I gave Eloise and Poppy a quick pet, then took the key from Romeo.

"Smooth move with the scissors," Maximus said. "Those guys never noticed a thing."

I grinned. "Hopefully he won't notice that missing key, either."

"Let's go before he does."

We're out of here, Romeo said. *We'll be back if we think you need us.*

"Thanks, guys. Your timing was impeccable. No way we'd have pulled that off so smoothly without you."

Romeo grinned and saluted, a little move that was becoming his signature. Poppy and Eloise grinned toothily. Then the three of them disappeared.

"As good as cat burglars, those three," Maximus said.

"They learned from the best." The thought of the Cats of Catastrophe made me smile. "Now let's get to that mountain."

We set off through the town, moving at a fast jog since no one could see us. Once we were visible again, we'd have to move sedately like everyone else to avoid eliciting suspicion.

When we ran through the square, it was just as busy as it had been, though no one seemed to be enjoying themselves. The old man was still there, but he didn't look toward us. Instead, he smiled blissfully off into the distance.

We made it through the rest of the town while our invisibility potion still worked. The mountain loomed in the distance, looking creepy as hell with the lightning striking behind it. I wondered if Hades minded the symbol of Zeus's power being present in his realm. Maybe he didn't have a choice.

We kept to a quick jog as we ran across the field, away from the village. My skin began to tingle and warm as the invisibility potion disappeared. When it left entirely, I turned back to see how far we were from the village. The settlement was just a few twinkly lights in the distance. No one would see us.

"That feels better." Maximus shook himself. He was still semitransparent from the death potion that we'd taken, but otherwise, he looked normal.

"No kidding."

A moment later, my comms charm buzzed to life, and Ana's voice echoed from it. "Rowan, are you there?"

"I'm here."

"Awesome. Wasn't sure if comms would work while you're in the Underworld. We're making good progress on the spells that will bind the Titans, but we need an update on your progress."

"We're close, I think. Nearly to Hecate's realm."

"Good. Because we need you to hurry. Things are getting worse. The dark magic is increasing so much that violence has broken out in the dark magic parts of the world. They were places that were already prone to it, so they're falling first. But regular places are getting bad, too. The police radios in the human realm are going nuts."

"Oh no."

"Yeah. There've even been a few deaths in riots that are linked to the growth of dark magic."

My heart plummeted. *Deaths?*

Shit. "We're on it."

"Great. If you can find them, we'll be ready to take them out. But be safe, okay?"

"Will do. And you too. Love you."

"Love you back."

I cut the comms and picked up the pace, my breath coming fast as I tried to keep up with Maximus. We reached the bottom of the mountain, and I looked upward. The slope was made of slick black stone that appeared slippery. I leaned down to touch it.

Cold.

Shit. Like really cold.

I shook my hand and looked at Maximus. "Black ice."

He rubbed his face, a thoughtful expression creasing his brow. "I've got something for that."

His magic flared briefly on the air, a lovely scent of cedar amidst the strangely smoky smell of the icy mountain. Gloves appeared in his hands, then the spikey things that went on the bottom of shoes, and finally two ice picks. He handed a set to me, and I took them gratefully.

"Thanks."

"Anytime."

We set about putting on our cold weather gear, strapping the spikes to the bottoms of our shoes and tugging on the gloves.

Then we began to climb. It was awkward at first, and I slipped despite the spikes. Maximus didn't, of course.

I glanced at him. "Have a lot of practice with this?"

"Some. Did a job in the Alps a few years ago."

"Cool." My foot slipped, but I was speedy with the pick, swinging it into the ice. It caught fast, and I pulled myself up.

I became steadier and quicker by the halfway point, finally getting into the swing of things. Pun intended. I grinned.

My heart thundered from exertion and my face warmed. I didn't dare touch the unnaturally cold ice with my bare skin, no matter how hot I was getting.

"We're nearing the top," Maximus said a while later.

Panting, I looked up, spotting the peak. There was a huge gate, locked up tight against interlopers. I couldn't see the guards, but they were probably there. A few yards away, there was a rock outcropping that would hide us from them.

I pointed to it. "Let's change back there."

Maximus nodded, and we climbed up toward it, finding a little nook with a semi-flat surface to stand on. I braced myself against Maximus and reached into my potion belt.

"Wait." Maximus reached for my hand, stopping it.

I looked up, surprised. "What's wrong? Don't want to become the judge?"

Our plan was to use my glamour potion to shift into the forms of the judges and stroll past the guards. That's what the hairs were for.

"No, that's fine." His eyes met mine. The heat in his gaze made me warm. "Just want to look at you one last time before you grow a beard. Maybe steal a kiss."

My interest piqued and my heart rate sped up. "Oh, really?"

"Really."

"If it's quick." Though I didn't want it to be quick, that was for sure. But this really wasn't the place for any long-lasting canoodling.

Maximus leaned down and pressed his lips to mine. They were firm and soft at the same time, warm and amazing. I moaned, leaning into him.

He gave my bottom lip one quick nip—just enough to get my heart really going—then pulled back.

"See?" He raised his hands. "Quick, like I promised."

"Too quick." I grinned, reaching into my pocket. "Not just because it was a great kiss, but because now we have to eat one of these gross hairs."

Maximus grimaced and nodded, reaching into his pocket for

his own little cluster of hair. My stomach lurched slightly as I stared at it, but I shook it away.

Has to be done.

I grabbed the tiny vial of potion from my belt and handed it to Maximus. Then I took another and uncorked it, raising it to him. "Cheers."

"Cheers." He popped the hair in his mouth, then threw back the potion.

I did the same, grimacing as I swallowed. Pain shot through my limbs as I shifted, and my jeans and leather jacket transformed into the robe that Aeacus had worn. There was something dangling between my legs, and it was *weird*.

I grimaced. Ew. Balls.

They were just dandy on men, but I'd never coveted a pair for myself, and now that I had them, it was definitely weird. I'd used this potion before, but I'd always transformed into a guy who wasn't freeballing it, apparently. This was way more...obvious.

I turned my mind from the juvenile thoughts and studied Maximus, who suddenly looked like a grizzled old judge. "Gotta say, I prefer the original you."

A smile tugged at the corner of his mouth, and it was weird because I could almost see him beneath the facade. "Likewise. Ready to go?"

"Let's get this over with. The potion won't last more than thirty minutes, I don't think. Hour at most."

He nodded, and we began to climb. Once again, my heart rate started going and my thighs began to burn. Near the top, it began to level out, and we were able to chuck our equipment. I had a feeling that the judges didn't use modern ice-climbing gear.

I tried to make my stride confident as I walked toward the gates, but my new masculine accessories made it weird.

Maximus didn't have any trouble with that, of course. It felt different to be a dude, though. I'd never had a ladylike walk, but I tried to give this one some extra testosterone.

The gates loomed ahead of us, carved of solid black wood with decorative elements that looked a lot like skulls, all piled on top of each other. Writing was carved over the gate, and I squinted at it, translating.

"Beware all who enter the domain of Hecate," I read.

"Fantastic. Sounds like fun."

"Judges!" The masculine voice sounded from the top of the gate, and I looked up.

A guard stood there, dressed in black metal armor with a feather sticking out of his helmet that looked like it'd come from a possessed demon ostrich.

Fancy.

I raised my hand in a half-hearted acknowledgment, pretending that I was very important and busy. That had to be how the judges acted normally, right?

Made sense to me, at least.

"Where is your carriage?" the guard shouted.

Carriage. So that's how they got up here.

"Broken," Maximus shouted up. "We decided to walk."

"Walk?" The confusion was clear in the guard's face. If I'd been able to see him clearly, he'd probably look like a golden retriever trying to understand English.

"Yes, walk." Maximus made his voice hard.

I strode toward the door, digging the key out of my pocket. We definitely needed to get away from the curious and dumb guard.

The lock was a heavy metal affair that quickly swallowed the key. I cranked it right, and magic sparked around the lock.

Please open.

Finally, it *snicked.*

I removed the key and stepped back as the gate began to rise, magic hauling it upward. There wasn't a single rope or pulley that I could see, but the thing rose all the same.

Maximus joined me, and as the gate lifted, dark magic rolled out of Hecate's realm. It reeked of dead bodies and crawled across my skin like bugs.

Holy fates, what are we walking into?

CHAPTER NINE

Hecate's realm spread out before us, and I blinked.

Was that a road made of lava?

Holy fates, it was.

It wound down the mountain, a bright red path that bubbled and swirled. I could only tell it was a road because a black carriage sat upon it, pulled by two skeletal horses. They were nothing but bleached white bones with fire for eyes, and they stomped their hooves impatiently, clearly waiting.

For us?

The area on either side of the road was covered in sharp black glass. Obsidian.

Maximus nodded toward it. "No way we can walk on that."

"No." I looked up at the guard, who watched us expectantly.

If the judges normally brought a carriage up here, would they get in this one?

Yes. Because Elysium wasn't the kind of place to have demon skeleton horses that could walk on lava. It was more of a real horse and happy afterlife sort of place. I'd bet money that the judges left their Elysium ride on that side of the gate and hopped onto the hell carriage on this side.

"Let's get in," I said.

Maximus started forward, walking only on the section of flat ground that wouldn't tear our shoes and feet to pieces.

The horses sidled closer to the flat ground, and he climbed up into the carriage without touching the lava.

I followed, the heat from below billowing up to warm my legs. Sweat broke out on my back at the idea of falling into the molten rock, and I made sure to get a good grip on the carriage. Maximus reached for me, drawing back when he saw that I had it. Probably didn't want to give the guard a show.

Once I was settled, I murmured, "How the hell do we drive this thing?"

Fortunately, the horses picked up the pace right away, knowing just where to go. They clomped away over the lava, their hooves sending up little sprays of it.

How the hell were they walking on it without being swallowed up and burned? And the carriage?

I'd seen a lot of cool magic in my day, but this topped it.

"Could this be more over the top?" Maximus asked.

I surveyed the jagged black glass and the lava river, my gaze landing on the horses' skulls. "No. Or yeah, maybe. But only if Satan were the butler."

"I wouldn't be surprised."

I grinned. "Me neither."

The heat from below was making me sweat, though I had a feeling it wasn't quite as hot as normal lava.

We were halfway down the mountain when I saw the city in the distance. The buildings were all black, blending so perfectly with the night that it was almost difficult to see them. A full moon glowed overhead, and I got the feeling that it was always full here. Maybe always night, too.

After all, Hecate was a goddess of night and the moon. Different from Artemis in a big way, though.

The buildings of the city rose high into the sky, ancient structures made of black marble that had sat here for thousands of years. A fiery river passed in front of the city. At first I thought it was also made of lava, but the flames flickered high.

"The Phlegethon," Maximus said. "One of the five rivers in hell, and the one that leads to Tartarus."

I swallowed hard. "Perfect, I love being close to those monsters."

Oh fates, I hoped we wouldn't run into any Titans. The ones on earth were enough to deal with.

We were still at least a mile from the city when I began to hear the baying of hounds. I shivered.

"They don't sound happy," Maximus said.

"No, they sound pissed." I imagined Cerberus.

Please don't be a bunch of Cerberuses.

I'd seen those dogs in the symbol of Hecate though. They must be a big deal to her. The carriage rolled ever forward, and my skin began to prickle as we neared. The dark magic that had nearly bowled me over earlier hit me even harder.

"Ugh, Hecate has some ugly magic," I muttered.

Maximus grimaced. "Smells like rotten flesh."

I didn't ask how he knew what that smelled like. I knew. Enough time with the wounded at the Colosseum and he probably had a real good idea.

The gate to the city was smaller than the one at the top of the mountain, but it was still an impressive affair. It was built of dark black wood and decorated with iron spikes that looked suspiciously rusty. Almost like blood coated them.

I shuddered. Would my key work on that? Because I really didn't want to climb that gate.

Movement at the top caught my eye. Two guards stood there, each dressed identically to the first ones we'd seen on the mountaintop. They, too, wore demon ostrich feathers, a fancy topping to their deadly armor and weapons.

I raised my hand in a half-hearted "I'm here" greeting that I figured busy, important people favored.

The guards seemed to like it, because the gates to the city rolled open.

"Nicely done," Maximus said.

"I think I'm getting used to this." Except I had to look like an old man to get these privileges, and that really wasn't worth it.

The horses carried us through the gates and onto a black cobblestone road that twisted between the tall stone buildings. The buildings were constructed with dozens of columns, each with flaming black rose vines twining around the marble.

The horses took us to a main square in town where a fountain shot fire into the air. Four huge buildings bordered the square, and all had the empty, daunting look of ancient office buildings.

What needed administration in hell, though? Torture? Black magic?

The horses stopped abruptly, and I shifted forward in my seat.

I threw out my hands to catch myself, then looked at Maximus. "Ride's over, I think."

He nodded and jumped down gracefully. I followed, nearly getting caught up in my robes.

As soon as we were out of the carriage, the horses picked up their hooves and moved on, clip-clopping around the fountain and off up the street.

Maximus grabbed my hand. "Let's find a place for recon."

"Couldn't agree more." We were going to lose this glamour soon, and I didn't want to be hanging around in the open as I shifted back into my normal self.

Together, we hurried toward the corner of the square. We

tucked ourselves back into the entrance of an alley and surveyed the square we'd left behind. It was nearly empty, with only a few faded souls wandering through. They were as ghostly as the figures in Elysium had been, but there were two that were more solid. Whether they were dead or alive, I had no idea.

"This place is huge," I said.

"We'll just follow the most disgusting magic. Since Hecate rules this place, she'll probably be at the end of it."

It'd work, I bet.

Except for the fact that I was feeling good magic right now. "Do you feel that? The light magic?"

Maximus frowned. "A bit. What's it doing here though?"

"Don't get me wrong, this place feels like a collision of dark magic fireworks. But I'm definitely getting a hint of light magic." I spun in a circle, searching for it. "It's so out of place."

"It's not us?"

"No. But we should be careful to control our signatures. It's different. And almost familiar." I blinked, squinting at an alley about fifteen yards away. A cloaked figure watched us.

"Come on." I grabbed Maximus's hand and pulled him down the street.

We passed a shadowy person who looked down at our joined hands.

Shit.

We looked like the two old judges still. And I'd bet big bucks they didn't hold hands. Too grouchy to hold hands with anyone.

I dropped Maximus's grip, but I didn't look away from the figure. Who the hell was it?

As we neared, I felt the magic of the glamour potion begin to wear off. I shivered as it went, wanting to see the person before I revealed myself.

"Judge." The voice rasped like a phone sex operator with a pack-a-day habit.

I blinked. "Mordaca?"

Now that I looked at the figure, the hood rose unnaturally high on the head. Her magic burned at the back of my throat, the taste of good whiskey.

I couldn't see the figure's eyes, but I could feel her confusion. "Rowan?"

"Yes. You can sense my magic?"

"I'm good at sensing magic, even suppressed magic." She dropped her hood, blinking at us from behind her mask of dark eye makeup. Her blood red lips parted on a confused smile, and I realized this was the first time I'd ever seen her without fifty percent of her tits on display. The robe covered her from head to foot, and she was clearly on some kind of secret mission.

"What are you doing here?" I asked.

"Why do you look like that?" She squinted at us.

"I won't look like this for long." The glamour was really starting to tingle now. "Let's get back into the alley."

Mordaca stepped back without asking questions. We followed her into the alley, making it into the shadows just as the glamour fell away entirely. Maximus returned to his normal self, and I almost sighed with pleasure. Damn, he looked good.

I peeked down at myself, pleased to see that I looked normal, then up at Maximus. "How's my face."

"Beautiful as ever."

"Quit flirting and tell me why you're in this godsforsaken hellhole."

I turned toward Mordaca. "Tell me why *you're* here."

"Okay, we'll trade. But you go first."

"Promise to reciprocate?"

She scowled. "Promise."

"We're looking for Hecate. It has to do with—"

"Saving the world?" she cut in.

"Well, basically, yeah."

"You're in the right place, then." She pointed to something over my head. "Follow those symbols to the crossroads, then take the stairs down."

I turned to look up at a symbol of two dogs and two torches. The torches were crossed, and the dogs stood on either side.

"It's her crest," Mordaca said. "You'll find her if you follow it. And once you're in her underground lair, your transport charm won't work. I assume that's how you plan to get out of here?"

I patted my pocket, where the stone was tucked away. "Yes."

"Get out of there before you use it. They'll only work on the surface." Her eyes turned shadowed, as if she'd learned the hard way.

"Thank you." That little bit of info would probably save our lives. "So, why are you here?"

"That's my business."

"You promised to share."

She scowled and her eyes shot daggers. "Fine. I'm looking for Aerdeca."

"Why is she here?"

"I never promised to reveal *her* secrets."

"Wiley," Maximus said.

"Very." She grinned, her teeth glinting white in the shadows.

"What do you want us to do if we happen to find her?" I asked.

"You won't." She sounded so confident that I let it lie there.

"Good luck, then."

She nodded. "You as well."

I turned to go back to the street. As much as I wanted to grill her, this was the boundary of our friendship. She was clearly in some deep shit, but so was I. We'd help each other when we could, but right now, we each needed to help ourselves.

We were a few steps away when her voice echoed through the alley. "Rowan?"

I turned back.

"If you meet her, be tough. She respects that."

"I'm always tough."

"I know. And her pride is her weakness. Get her there."

I nodded. "Thanks. Let me know if you need any help with Aerdeca."

Her face softened, just briefly, and she looked like an entirely different person.

For the briefest moment, I realized that Mordaca wore a mask. Not just the thick sweep of black around her eyes or the crazy hair or blood red lipstick. But *her*.

I didn't know Mordaca at all, I realized. Probably no one did. No one except Aerdeca.

I turned away, leaving her to it. But when I was back on earth, and they were, too, I'd figure out who the heck she was. Not just to sate my curiosity, but because I had a feeling I'd really like her.

"That was odd," Maximus said as we stepped back into the main square.

"No kidding." I searched for the symbol, my gaze finally landing on a stone carving on the side of a building. "There."

We went to it, almost immediately spotting another one a little farther down.

"This won't be so hard," Maximus said.

"Famous last words." I grinned as we continued through the square, following the symbols onto a busy road.

There were more skeletal carriages there, and the black buildings looked like they were shops. Horrible things were for sale, of course, and it reminded me of The Vaults back in Edinburgh.

Dark magic reeked in this place, and I couldn't wait to get out of here. We passed by shadowy wraiths who looked downright miserable, as well as others who wore evil smiles. There were demons, too, and the flickering fires in the streetlights glinted off fangs and scales. I stuck close to Maximus, hoping that our semitransparent forms helped us blend in. Our modern clothes weren't doing us any favors.

Two demons spilled out of a pub that blasted with the sound of drums and some kind of screeching that made my hair stand on end. The demons went for each other like rabid dogs, swinging broken bottles and going for the neck.

Maximus and I darted out of the way and kept going, narrowly avoiding a fight. Those two had the look of drunks who would brawl with anyone, and I wasn't going to volunteer.

"Nice place," Maximus muttered.

"Peachy."

The next street we came to was more residential, but the dark magic in the air made my stomach turn.

The sounds of hounds picked up again, and I frowned. "What's with all the dogs? Where *are* they?"

"Beats me. I can't see them."

When we reached the crossroads, I stopped dead. "This has to be it."

Where the two roads intersected, black magic sparked. It glittered in the air, bringing with it an even stronger stench of rotten flesh.

Maximus grimaced. "We're definitely close."

I pointed to an archway across the road, sitting at the corner of the crossroads. Hecate's symbol was carved into the stone. "Bet you twenty bucks there are stairs under that arch."

"Not taking that bet." He grabbed my hand, and we crossed the street, hurrying in front of a carriage that picked up pace when it saw us, aiming to run us over.

I flipped the driver off, a demon with green fangs.

He just smiled wider.

"Dick," I muttered.

Maximus chuckled and pointed to the arch. "I'm glad I didn't take that bet."

Jackpot. A wide set of stairs led down into the darkness. Torches burned on either side, and I shivered.

"It looks like something from nightmares." I gave my voice my best witchy impression. "Come, come, down into the dark."

Maximus wrapped an arm around my shoulders. "I've got you, babe."

I grinned up at him. "You copping a feel?"

"Would you object?"

"With you, no. But I think I've made my feelings quite clear, so it wouldn't be copping, technically."

"Just responding to an invitation?"

"Exactly."

"I RSVP yes."

I laughed at the terrible joke. "Watch a lot of wedding shows when you were learning about the modern day?"

"A few." He shuddered. "I learned what a bridezilla is."

"Charming, huh?"

"Very."

I wanted to joke like this forever, but we were literally in hell on a visit to the almost-devil, so now was not the time. "Let's go."

We started down, going side by side into the dark. As we descended, the baying of hounds became louder.

"They're down here?" Maximus asked.

"I think they might be everywhere."

We were deep underground by the time the stairs leveled out in a room that was about thirty feet by thirty feet. Hecate's symbol was etched into the ground, and an archway of flame stood on the other side. We'd have to walk through fire to keep going.

I swallowed hard. "Fantastic."

Maximus walked toward the flame, holding out his hand.

LINSEY HALL

Slowly, he moved it closer to the flickering orange fire. "It's not hot."

"Let's go, then."

Together, we walked through the flame. I couldn't help the spike of adrenaline that hit me—it really *looked* like fire—so I closed my eyes.

Just as Maximus had said, it didn't burn.

I opened my eyes on the other side and gasped. "Holy fates."

"There have to be thousands." Maximus's gaze ran over the enormous crowd in the huge underground atrium. The ceiling was high, and though the room was enormous, the crush of bodies was intense.

"They're all wearing identical cloaks," I said. The red fabric draped over their forms, concealing them entirely.

"Hang on." Maximus's magic barely flared as he conjured two cloaks for us.

I threw mine over my shoulders and pulled up the hood. Maximus did the same, and I reached for his hand, determined not to let go. If I lost him in this crush, I'd never find him again.

"What can you see up there?" I asked. I might have super good eyesight, but he had the height. And in here, that was everything.

"Looks like there's an exit on the other side, through a big arch. There's a smaller group in front of it."

"Let's join them."

He nodded and began to pull me through the crowd. As we pushed through, I realized that all the individuals were chanting something low under their breath. It was almost as if this were a worship session, but everyone was doing it on their own.

Praying to Hecate? Or someone else?

I couldn't quite understand what they were saying. The words were too foreign or jumbled. How were they speaking, though? In Elysium, no one had been able to speak without an offering of blood.

Maybe that was why they worshipped her.

A cloaked figure slammed into us, tearing my hand away from Maximus. My heart leapt into my throat, and I bit back a scream.

"Maximus!" I whispered, reaching out for him.

The figure who'd slammed into us surged toward me, getting right in my face. Beneath the cloak, I could see crazed blue eyes and a vacant grin. He was semi-ghostly, just like we were.

The figure reached for my neck, hissing, "Invader."

"No." I smacked his hands away, but he thrust them back at me. Panic trilled along my spine.

If everyone here realized that we were interlopers, we were dead. No way we could fight them all. The figure wrapped strong hands around my neck and squeezed.

I might've looked dead because of the potion, but I sure as heck wasn't. My neck ached and my lungs burned as he cut off my air.

Oh fates, he could kill me.

CHAPTER TEN

Quickly, I drew a dagger from the ether and shoved it into his stomach.

Please work.

The figure opened his mouth as if to scream, and I smacked a hand over his lips, grimacing at the slimy feel. Ew.

I twisted the knife, jerking it upward.

The figure crumpled.

My blade slipped out as he fell, and I looked up, desperately searching for Maximus. He pushed his way past two people, stopping right in front of me.

"He could sense we were different." My heart still pounded in my ears.

"Let's hurry, then." Maximus grabbed my hand again. This time, his grip was almost punishingly tight, but I squeezed back even harder.

We slipped through the crowd, trying to keep the shoving to a minimum. No need to draw attention.

By the time we neared the small group in front of the arch, I was panting. Despite the high ceiling, this place felt insanely claustrophobic. All around, people pushed and jostled, excited for something. Occasionally, I saw flashes of the people beneath the cloaks. All were ghostly, and all had the intense eyes of the man who'd attacked me.

It was a cult. Some kind of weird dark magic death cult.

And their leader was the one I was supposed to convince to give us world-saving info.

Yeah, that'd be easy.

Flames burst to life in the middle of the archway, briefly flaring a bright blue. The energy in the crowd rose, and excited murmurs filtered through.

Maximus's grip on my hand tightened. I held my breath, waiting. The anticipation in the air was impossible to ignore, and even I started to feel a bit excited.

I took it as more evidence that I had an unnatural affinity for this place. No matter how hard I wanted to get rid of the darkness inside me, it was always there.

Just my freaking luck.

The flames flared bright purple, and the crowd surged forward. Maximus and I didn't even have a choice. We were carried through on a wave of bodies, flowing with the crowd toward the purple flames. My heart thundered as we neared, and I struggled to move backward, to have some control of our destination. Maximus pulled back as well, but the crush of bodies was too powerful. They forced us through the flames, which reeked of sulfur and prickled against my skin as we passed.

Thank fates they didn't burn.

We entered a room that was far smaller than the one we'd been in. The ceiling was about thirty feet high, and it was a narrow space, over a hundred feet long. On the far end rose a stone platform. A waterfall poured down from behind it, sparkling with dark magic. The crowd surged toward it, beginning to chant. Their words were unfamiliar, which meant they weren't Greek, since I could now understand it. There were possibly some Greek root words, but this was some dark hell language.

The crowd stopped abruptly in front of the waterfall, leaving about twenty feet between them and the platform with the water pouring down behind it. Maximus and I stood right in the middle of them, pressed together.

Hounds began to howl, baying toward a moon I couldn't see. I looked around, searching for them, but saw only the crowd of ghosts with feverish eyes.

"Where the hell are they?" Maximus murmured.

"No idea."

The waterfall flared with dark magic, catching my attention. I turned toward it, unconsciously leaning forward with the rest of the crowd.

Whatever they were waiting for was about to happen.

A moment later, a tall figure stepped through the waterfall, her dark hair flowing down her back. Two tall dogs stood at her side, each skinny with sleek black fur and red eyes. They stood on the stone stage, staring out at the crowd.

The woman was beautiful in a cruel way, with thin lips and dark eyes. Her dress was a glorious purple sheath of silk, with flowing sleeves trimmed in gold.

Damn, Hecate could dress.

Her magic reeked of sulfur and rotten vegetables, and the smile that she shot the crowd was both satisfied and devious. She definitely liked being worshiped. With the way this crowd was nearly vibrating with excitement, they liked worshipping her.

Pride. That was her thing, according to Mordaca.

Her dark gaze traveled over the worshippers and stopped on Maximus and me. Her eyes widened.

Well, there went our cover.

I'd hoped to observe her for longer, but it looked like that wasn't going to happen.

"Intruders." She pursed her lips and tilted her head. "Well, isn't that interesting."

My heart began to thud. If she decided to sic her minions on us, we were in trouble. I tensed, ready to fight.

She looked down at her dogs. "Brutus? Judas? What do you think?"

They woofed. I had no idea what it meant, but she seemed to like it, because she smiled and raised her hands to make a parting-the-waters gesture. The crowd surged back from us, forming a ring with us at the center. There was about twenty feet between me and the nearest cult member, but somehow, this felt even more claustrophobic. Everyone stared at us, their interest palpable.

The dark waterfall shimmered, and twenty transparent blue figures stepped out from beneath the water, flanking Hecate like an army.

My heart leapt into my throat and my skin turned to ice.

Phantoms.

Oh, shit.

Shit, shit, shit.

I wanted to turn and run—anyone in their right mind would turn and run.

Phantoms were literally the worst supernatural creatures out there, and it didn't surprise me a bit that Hecate would have an army of them. The ghostly figures fed on the misery and fear of their victims, forcing them to relive everything terrible in their lives.

Why the hell were they here?

Though I asked the question, I had a sinking feeling that I knew.

It was nearly impossible to fight Phantoms. Del, the FireSoul who was half Phantom, could go up against them when she was in her Phantom form. But they were so incorporeal that I couldn't make contact with them in my human form.

But if they got a grip on me...

I shuddered.

Hecate said nothing, just raised her hands and gestured like a flight attendant pointing down the aisle toward the exit at the back. She looked like an icy cold bitch, and I swallowed hard.

The Phantoms surged forward, a wave of transparent blue figures. They were on us in an instant, their cold hands grasping. A strong grip tightened on my arm, and the touch nearly made my knees buckle. Pain shot through me as my mind exploded with agony.

Images of my sisters dying at the hands of the Titans flashed in my head, making tears spring to my eyes. Thoughts of me succumbing to the darkness within me followed close on its heels.

I would become a slave to the darkness and forsake my sisters, resulting in their deaths. Resulting in the destruction of the Protectorate. The death of Maximus.

Memories of my time with the Rebel Gods surged within me. I'd succumbed to their darkness during my captivity.

I was prone to it.

I could do it again.

I *would* do it again.

The horrible thoughts tumbled around in my head as the Phantoms reached for me, their hands scrabbling against my limbs.

I sucked in a ragged breath, trying to get control of myself. I couldn't fail like this, a victim to my own worst fears.

Beside me, Maximus struck out.

His hand connected with a Phantom's cheek, and the creature flung backward.

Wait, what?

Maximus had been able to hurt the Phantoms.

Because we were also kind of ghostly?

Maybe.

I'd take it.

As the terrible thoughts threatened to drag me down into despair, I swung my fist toward the nearest monster. My hand connected with its cheek, and the creature stumbled backward.

Hell yeah.

The little victory gave me hope, and funnily enough, that hope was enough to light a fire within me. Horrible images still flowed through my mind, making me shake, but I had enough strength to lash out.

I went wild, kicking and punching. It was like a demon took over my body, fueled by panic and terror. There was nothing worse than being trapped in my own fears, and I'd do anything to get out of it.

The Phantoms began to stumble back, my attack more than they could take. Next to me, Maximus fought off his own demons, and they were surging backward even faster than mine were.

"Enough!" Hecate's voice echoed through the chamber.

The Phantoms stopped, but I didn't. I charged them.

When I came back to my senses, the idea that I'd charged them would sound insane. But I couldn't help it.

I was sick of being afraid. *Sick of it.*

Sick of my horrible memories, sick of my fear of falling to the darkness, sick of my fear of not being good enough.

So I went nuts, going after the Phantoms like I was going to tear them limb from limb.

"I said, *enough!*" Hecate's voice thundered through the room, and my limbs froze in place.

I was in mid punch, my arm outstretched. I could even feel

the snarl on my face. But I was frozen solid. Though I couldn't even move my eyes, I could just barely make out the image of Hecate staring at me. The Phantoms were frozen all around, some of them running, some of them looking like they wanted to charge me, their hands outstretched and their faces twisted in hungry grimaces.

Bring it! I wanted to shout.

"Come." Hecate's icy voice cracked through the room, and the Phantoms followed the command, drifting back to stand behind her.

My limbs unfroze, and I almost fell over. At the last second, I caught myself, staying on my feet. Panting, I stared at Hecate, hating her with everything in my soul.

Then I turned and went back to Maximus, who looked pale beneath his hood. His jaw was tense and his eyes shadowed. He'd probably just relived his time in the Colosseum, or something even worse. I wanted to reach for him. To comfort him.

It wasn't an option right now. Revealing weakness was the worst thing we could to.

So I stopped next to him, pressing my shoulder to his. It was the most we could manage, and it helped. Warmth spread through me, his touch grounding me. He was my anchor in the storm, and I hoped I was his.

I turned to face Hecate.

"Who are you?" Hecate demanded. "And what are you doing in my domain, uninvited?"

"I don't suppose you'd believe we want to join your cult?" I almost put the word *weird* in front of cult, but bit it back at the last minute. I'd seen what she was capable of, and I didn't want to mess with her.

"You could only wish to be so lucky as to join my minions."

I glanced around to see how the crowd liked being called

minions, but there was just an audible sigh of happiness from this bunch.

Oookay.

Weirdos.

"Who are you?" Her voice cracked like a whip.

I drew back my hood to reveal my face. "I am Rowan Blackwood, the Greek Dragon God."

Her brows rose. "Ah, so you are the one."

I nodded.

"Well, I didn't give you my magic."

No, and I was glad. Only some of the Greek gods had volunteered, and I was having enough of a problem with Hades's magic that I didn't want her dirty stuff as well.

I shrugged. "Fine by me."

She scowled, then seemed to realize she was showing emotion, and smoothed out her features. "I don't think I like you."

I resisted a second shrug, and I definitely didn't say that I didn't like her either.

"And who's the big fellow with you?" she purred.

Maximus drew back his hood, and she stared at him appreciatively.

Ha. She might've wanted him, but he was mine.

"I am Maximus Valerius."

"Ah, gladiator. I followed your exploits in the Colosseum years ago."

Of course she had a thing for enforced blood sports. What a bitch.

He nodded, but said nothing and appeared to be supremely bored. Despite the pain of what we'd just gone through, he was determined to piss her off. Mordaca had said "be tough," and he had no problem with that. I nearly grinned. Her pride would *not* like that.

"Well, neither of you are weak. Why are you here?"

"We have questions," I said.

"Why would I answer them?"

"Maybe you can't."

"I can do anything."

"Really?" I tried to make my voice skeptical. She clearly wasn't going to give me the info I wanted because I asked nicely. So I had to trick her into it. Or win it from her.

"Of course I can." She scoffed.

"Better than me?"

She looked at me like I was crazy. Maybe I was.

"Are you challenging me?" she demanded.

I nodded. "Yeah. A competition. Something fair, but difficult. If I win, you give me the info I want. If you win, I'll leave."

"If I win, you'll join my minions."

Oh, hell no. That would *not* be happening. "What did you have in mind?"

She turned around and swept her arm out. The Phantoms disappeared, and so did the waterfall and platform upon which she stood. Suddenly, she was at my level.

The minions around us gasped and stepped back. Suddenly, there was no one standing between me and Hecate.

The underground cavern expanded, and a massive lake appeared in its place. It had to be the size of four football fields put together, and the water gleamed black. The stench of sulfur was nearly unbearable. I breathed shallowly through my mouth, nearly gagging.

Hecate turned back to me. "A little competition."

I grimaced. "I'm not swimming in that."

"No, you certainly aren't. It's acid, and if you fell in, you'd die."

Oh, fantastic.

"We will, however, race to get across." She swept her hand

toward the ground, and two wooden rafts appeared. "You will go alone. The gladiator stays on the shore. The first one to the other side, wins."

I swallowed hard, stepping forward. Maximus' brow was furrowed and his eyes worried. He clearly didn't like this, but Hecate wouldn't budge.

"Fine." I looked at Maximus, who nodded at me.

"You can do this."

"Thanks." I pressed a quick kiss to his lips, not giving a damn that I had an audience of two dozen minions and one seriously bitchy goddess.

I strode toward Hecate, eyeing the shitty little raft with dismay. It looked flimsy as hell.

Hecate's magic surged again, and a long paddle appeared. "Because I'm feeling generous."

"Thanks." I didn't sound thankful though.

She didn't have a paddle, which probably meant she had something up her sleeve.

I stopped at the edge of the water, where it lapped against the shore. Gingerly, I stuck the very tip of my boot in. Just a couple millimeters of the toe. It hissed and sizzled, eating away at the sole.

Shit. I jerked my foot back.

Yeah, she wasn't kidding about this *die if you fall in* bit.

Hecate grinned evilly, then turned to the dogs, who'd stuck by her side every second. "Brutus, Judas. You may play."

The dog's fiery eyes lit with joy, and they leapt up, skinny limbs flashing, then spun and sped into the water. They barked with joy, splashing around in the sulfurous acid. True hellhounds. They played for a few seconds, then trotted up through the shallows, headed for Hecate's raft.

They reached it and went immediately for the two ropes that I only now noticed, picking them up in their jaws and tugging.

Oh, crap. They were going to pull her across.

I rushed to my raft and grabbed the long paddle. "We're starting now?"

"Fine." Her voice sounded bored, and she clearly thought her victory would be easy.

No way in hell. Even though we were already *in* hell.

I pushed my raft out onto the shallows, careful not to touch the water. When it was floating, I jumped on carefully, my heart leaping into my throat when the raft wobbled.

Oh, fates. This would be hard.

Gingerly, I put my paddle in the water and pushed myself forward. The raft glided over the stinking surface, which gleamed darkly. The stench made my eyes water, and I stared upward, blinking rapidly.

"Onward!" Hecate's voice sounded, and the dogs gave a joyful yip.

I turned back, spotting her standing on the raft to my left and looking like a queen, her dogs towing her along with big doggy grins on their faces.

I scowled and turned back, pushing my paddle as hard as I could. There had to be an easier way. Perhaps if I could control the water to push me along?

As if she'd heard my thought, Hecate shouted, "Wave!"

What the heck?

I turned to her, spotting her flourishing her hand at the water. As she'd commanded, a wave formed. It was small, but definitely big enough to tip me into the lake.

My skin chilled. Damn it.

I called on Poseidon's gift, feeling it swell inside me. I could feel the water as if it were part of myself, and since it was a stinking acidy mess, I shuddered.

There was no time to be grossed out. I used my power to command the water to flatten. My heart thundered as my magic went to work. The wave was nearly to me by the time it smoothed out. My raft rocked gently, and I crouched, bracing myself.

Sweat poured down my spine as the acidy water lapped at the edges of the raft.

Hecate was pulling into the lead now, her dogs dragging her faster than my oar could manage. I commanded the water to push me, but it barely worked. The raft had such a shallow draft that there was no surface for the water to push upon. I tried to create a current, but even that was nearly impossible in a lake.

Determined, I paddled faster, barely managing to keep up with Hecate. We were only a quarter of the way across when another wave came at me, this one bigger.

I called upon Poseidon's magic, barely managing to flatten the wave in time. My raft rocked, and I nearly went to my knees. All my fight training helped, and I kept paddling.

"So I see that Poseidon gave you his power," she said.

I didn't respond. My muscles ached and my eyes burned from the fumes of the water, but I gave it my all.

A wall of thorny vines grew up in front of me, at least five feet high and twenty feet across.

I hissed. "Not fair!"

"Life's not fair, honey, and this is my race."

I gritted my teeth. If I had to paddle around the wall, I'd lose any chance at winning. It'd just take too damned long.

No way in hell was I going to *lose.*

Not to this jerk, and not when so much was at stake. I held the paddle in one hand and dug into my potion bag with the other, then pulled out the familiar triangular-shaped disintegration bomb.

I hurled the thing at the wall, not bothering with careful aim. It was so big I'd hit it no matter what.

The potion bomb smashed into the thorny black vines, and

the wall began to disintegrate, falling into the water as dust. I paddled right over it, barely keeping up with Hecate.

She glared at me, dark eyes gleaming.

"That was all me," I said, referring to my potion genius.

She scowled, then looked at her dogs. "Faster, Brutus and Judas, faster!"

I dug my paddle into the water, giving it my all. Sweat slicked my hands, but I ignored it and gripped the paddle tighter.

Out of the corner of my left eye, I spotted Hecate waving her hand. Her magic swelled, the stench of rotten vegetables growing.

Ah, shit.

Frantically, my gaze passed over the water. What was she sending at me this time?

The water to my right surged. Another freaking wave?

She was a slow learner, if she thought I couldn't deal with that.

The wave grew.

Then two eyes appeared, peering above the water.

Ah, crap. Not a wave.

My heart jackhammered. The beast's head was two feet wide at least, with huge fangs and beady yellow eyes. It opened its mouth wider as it zipped toward me. I paddled faster, but I was only seventy percent of the way across, if that.

No way I could outrun this beast. And when it caught me, it'd knock me into the acid water.

Fear iced my spine. What the hell was I going to do?

CHAPTER ELEVEN

The sea monster swam faster, speeding toward me through the water. It was nearly to me, so close that I could see the glimmer of its dark green scales.

It opened its mouth wide and raised its head out of the water.

Crap!

I stopped paddling and faced the creature. It was only a few feet away, so I swung my paddle and smashed it in the face.

The creature fell back into the water, hissing, but it recovered quickly. It surged toward me again, fangs glinting. I poked it with my paddle, but it was too quick this time. The monster thrashed, jaws snapping at my paddle.

The wood splintered, and the beast chomped down, snapping it in half.

Crap!

"Oh, that's too bad!" Hecate said.

The sea monster chomped on the wood, eyeing my raft hungrily. It was coming for it next. Coming for me.

I nearly called a sword from the ether, but that would be too risky. I could barely move on the raft without upsetting it.

As if understanding what I needed, Zeus's lightning magic crackled within my veins. It lit me up like electricity.

But no, that wouldn't work. So far, I'd only been able to turn myself into a human lightning bolt. It worked well on land when I could wrap my arms around my prey. But I wasn't about to jump on that sea monster. If the acid water didn't get me, the electric shock in the water would.

No, I needed to be able to shoot a lightning bolt.

Bree had helped me in one training session, and while I hadn't mastered it, desperation was a damned powerful motivator.

The electricity sizzled within me, sparking along my skin and through my muscles. I focused on it, trying to draw it toward my center. *I* was in control here, not the god's magic.

The sea monster was finishing its wooden snack, and I was running out of time. I gathered up the magic that snapped within me, forcing it into a ball in my chest. My heart felt like it might explode.

I sucked in a deep breath and envisioned hurling my magic outward.

The sea monster charged again, only a dozen feet away.

I threw my magic at it, sending a lightning bolt straight from my chest and into the monster's face. The creature lit up like the Fourth of July, electricity frying its circuits.

The current traveled through the water, and Hecate's dogs gave a joyful yelp. There was no other word for the sound, and I shouldn't be surprised, given their love of the acid water.

As the sea monster sank beneath the surface, I looked over at the dogs, who were now swimming faster than ever. They'd used the electricity as fuel, and they were smoking my butt.

Damn it.

No way I could beat them. Especially not without an oar.

Hecate grinned and waved at me, now twenty feet ahead of

me. She was only about fifty feet from the shore, and if she kept going at that rate, I didn't have a chance.

I stared down at the broken oar in my hand. Even if Maximus could conjure me a new one all the way out here in the middle of the lake, I wouldn't be able to paddle fast enough to catch her.

Think. Think.

The dogs. They were my only option. To win, she had to stop moving forward, and I had to start moving—fast.

If I could get inside Cerberus's mind, I could do the same with her dogs. Two dogs wouldn't be easy, but I didn't have a choice.

I sucked in a deep breath and closed my eyes, focusing on the hounds. I could feel them, almost like I had radar inside my body and they were popping up, just ahead and to the left.

I called upon the gift that Artemis had given me, imagining my consciousness melding with the hound closest to me. I envisioned what it would be like to be him, and after a moment, my consciousness seemed to leave my body and join the dog's.

Boy, was he happy.

He loved this game. The acid pond was his favorite, so this was basically Christmas.

Okay, weirdo. You do you.

Except, wouldn't it be better if you were pulling the other raft? I asked him inside our minds.

He stopped abruptly, clearly confused.

Yep, I'm in your head. You're such a good boy. The best boy. Go push that other raft. It doesn't have ropes, but you can push it with your nose. It'll be so much fun.

He huffed a bit.

Come on, fella. You'll love it.

He huffed again, but finally dropped the rope clamped between his jaws.

Jackpot.

"What the hell?" Hecate's voice sounded, but the dog was already paddling away.

The dog and I were about twenty feet away. He was nearly to the raft and was so excited to get there that I felt confident enough to allow my consciousness to leave him. He'd keep going.

I allowed my consciousness to leave his and to join with the other dog's, and man, was this one confused. He kept looking between the shore and his buddy, who was paddling away toward my raft. My body stood stock-still on the raft in a state of stasis.

I'd better hurry, before Hecate figured out what was going on. It was dangerous to be out of my body like this. She could send something at me that I wasn't prepared to fight.

Good boy, I said to the dog from within his mind.

He perked up, and I could somehow sense—or feel—our tail wagging. He, too, liked to swim. But he *really* liked being called a good boy.

Hecate might be a bitch, but she was nice to her dogs. These guys seemed really happy.

"What the hell is going on?" she screeched.

Crap. I needed to pick up the pace.

Good boy, wouldn't it be fun to pull the other raft?

I could almost hear the dog shout *Yeah!*

I would have bet one million dollars that this dog was literally the worst guard dog in the history of time. If someone was nice to him, he loved them.

The dog dropped the rope and paddled off after his friend, making quick work of cutting through the acid water.

"Brutus! Judas! Get back here!" she shouted.

I rejoined my body just as the first dog reached the raft and began to push. The other joined shortly after. Hecate was scowling at me, her face so fierce that I thought she'd tear my head off if she could manage it.

"What have you done to my dogs?" she screeched.

"I have no idea what you're talking about." I grinned at her as we passed, the dogs pushing my raft quickly.

She had no paddle, so she was just standing there, staring. Her fists tightened, and I could all but feel the impotent rage. "You better not hurt them!"

Clearly, she wanted to smite me. Or command her dogs. But she was afraid to mess with whatever spell I'd cast. I didn't tell her it wasn't a spell, just a bit of suggestion made to two sweet but dumb dogs.

"Arghgh!" She conjured a paddle and began to row. "If you hurt them, I will tear you limb from limb and devour your entrails!"

I looked back at her. "I'm not going to hurt them!" I grinned. "But they do like me more."

Her face turned so red that I thought her head might pop right off her neck. Oh, fates. I probably shouldn't have said that.

My raft touched the other side of the lake and stopped abruptly. I stumbled slightly, then leapt off.

The dogs turned around and swam back to Hecate, who was nearly to the shore. They grabbed the ropes at the front of her boat and pulled her toward the shore, finishing their original job.

She jumped off and shot me one evil look, then bent and stared into her dogs' eyes. "Are you guys okay?"

Their tongues lolled out and they grinned, panting.

She stared hard at them. "You seem normal."

"They're fine. I just asked them for help."

She straightened and gave me a death glare. It would have withered a weaker person.

Maximus joined me, having walked around the edge of the lake while I was competing. "It looks like Rowan won."

Hecate hissed. "Fine. Come."

She stalked off, and I looked at Maximus. "She is *pissed.*"

He grinned, then pressed a quick kiss to my lips. "You did great."

"Thanks." I smiled, then turned and followed Hecate. She stalked off like she was going to kick some rowdy kids off her lawn.

Maximus and I followed her away from the lake, heading toward a darkened archway. Unlike the previous archways, this one was filled with a thick black smoke. The dogs bounded through, and Hecate followed at a more sedate pace, sailing through like a queen, leaving just a wisp of smoke behind her.

I looked up at Maximus. "She's a piece of work, eh?"

He nodded. "That's the truth."

I held my breath as we passed through the smoky arch, and it burned my eyes enough that I closed them. A few seconds later, I opened them and gasped.

I was in a library. And a graveyard.

What the heck?

I blinked, looking around with astonishment.

It was a massive round room, and with the exception of the space just in front of me, the entire perimeter was covered in loose black dirt and gravestones. Right ahead of me, at the far end of the room, a massive fireplace crackled with emerald fire. Tall bookshelves towered on either side, stuffed full of green- and purple-bound books. The chandelier hanging from the ceiling flickered with purple flame. Large green leather chairs were scattered through the space, and Hecate stalked toward one, then collapsed into it in a dramatic fashion.

She sighed heavily as she stared at us with bored eyes. The dogs bounded toward her, stopping briefly for a quick pet, before running right into the emerald flames in the massive fireplace.

"Well?" she said. "Can I offer you a drink? A snack, perhaps?"

I'd never heard anyone sound so annoyed in all my life. "Um, no thanks."

"Don't want to eat in the Underworld?"

"Not that it's not lovely here"—it wasn't—"but I don't think I want to stay for eternity."

She nodded. "I can't believe that idiot Persephone fell for it when Hades gave her the pomegranate seeds."

Eating the seeds had been the act that had gotten Persephone stuck here, but I'd thought Hecate was her handmaiden or something.

I resisted huffing out a dry laugh. It was silly of me to expect someone like Hecate to actually be respectful of her boss. Definitely not her style. And I doubted Persephone was a dummy. She probably knew the deal, but found Hecate to be useful.

"Well, what is it that you wanted to know?" Hecate twirled her dark hair around one fingertip, clearly trying to let us know that we were boring her.

"We're looking for the Stryx," I said. "We understand that they worship you, and Tiresias said that you would know where to find them. And maybe what their goal is in raising the Titans."

She nodded, an annoyed glint in her eyes. "Tiresias."

"He's never wrong." *So don't try to fake that you don't know.*

She scowled. "Fine. Yes. The Stryx worship me, as everyone clever does. And I'll tell you where they are, but I don't know that it will help you. Now that they've raised the Titans, they're impossible to defeat."

"We'll take care of that," Maximus said.

"Where are they?" I asked.

"They have a fortress on the island of Lektos, sixty miles off the coast of southern Greece. It is located directly beneath the Mage's Star. It's a place they built long ago, specifically for the Titans."

"They've been planning to raise them for a while?" I asked.

"Planning?" She laughed. "The Stryx aren't the ones in control, dear. The Titans are."

Cold fear raced down my spine. Until now, I'd considered the Titans to be weapons. Powerful weapons. Basically, nuclear weapons. But not the masterminds.

"What do you mean, exactly?" Maximus said.

"Just what I said. The Stryx are powerful witches. The Titans are essentially gods. And as they grow stronger, they take their rightful place."

Okay. Okay. Chill.

I should have expected something like this. I'd been so obsessed with the Stryx that I'd developed tunnel vision, but I didn't have to stay that way. Obviously, the Titans would be the bosses. They'd come out of Tartarus weak from their time in captivity, but their strength was growing.

"This fortress on Lektos, what's it like?" I asked.

She shrugged. "Big. Impossible to overtake. The walls are impenetrable."

She was so delighted when she said it that I believed her.

"By an army, you mean," Maximus said.

"Of course."

"But a smaller group could sneak in," he said.

"Perhaps. I've heard there's a tunnel under the water." She shrugged. "Could be an old wives' tale. But what is a small group going to do in there? They can't fight the Titans. Not as they continue to grow stronger. They'll be invincible soon."

"Their dark magic is growing," I said.

"Oh, yes." Hecate grinned. "So many more supernaturals

and humans are turning to the dark side than ever before. Why, in the last few days, the number of my worshippers has tripled."

Damn. "So you don't want me to stop the Titans or the Stryx."

"Of course not." She waved her hand dismissively. "But you won't be able to. I'm giving you your answers because you won our race, but I also don't think you'll actually be able to stop them. So no harm."

My jaw tightened. She'd be wrong about that. I'd make sure of it. "How is the Titans' dark magic growing? Where is it coming from? Is it because they're no longer bound by Tartarus?" That was Jude's running theory, at least, though we didn't really know.

"You're asking a lot more questions than we agreed to."

"We didn't agree to a specific number."

She sighed, her eyes flashing in annoyance. Her lips tightened. Yeah, she was getting peeved. She'd started out pissed, and it was only getting worse. When she spoke, it was reflected in her voice. "There's a common understanding of how many questions one gets to ask after succeeding in one measly challenge."

"So, if I wanted to ask more questions, I'd have to beat you at more challenges?"

"If I agreed to them, which I won't. Not after you stole my dogs. You may have won, but I don't like how you did it." Anger flickered in her eyes.

I needed to tread lightly. Pissing her off when we were this deep in her domain was a *bad* idea.

"How did you do it, by the way?" Hecate leaned forward. "Convince my dogs, I mean."

I grinned. "Artemis. She has the most amazing magic. I can communicate with animals."

Hecate huffed out a breath and sat back. "Oh, Artemis has the most amazing magic? Artemis?" She sounded *pissed*. Was there a history between her and Artemis I didn't understand? She shook her head. "Coming into my home. Taking my dogs. Then insulting me."

"It wasn't an insult!" *Uh-oh.*

"Oh, it wasn't? You come in here and say *to my face* that Artemis has the most amazing magic?" She shook her head. "I can't believe you."

"Not like, more amazing than yours," I said. Oh shit. I'd forgotten how fickle the gods could be. How obsessed they were with status and their petty grievances.

And Hecate's thing was her pride. I'd been *told*.

And still, I'd put my foot in my mouth. Shit.

Anger was vibrating around Hecate now, and we'd definitely reached a turning point. I glanced at Maximus, whose muscles were tense. He was ready to move.

He met my gaze and nodded.

Time to get out of here.

"Thank you for the answers." I stood. "We should be going now."

"Oh, I think you should be." She stood, raising her arms. The emerald fire flared bright behind her, and the purple-flame chandelier popped with light. The two colors were reflected in her eyes, and her face took on a crazed expression. Her dark hair began to float around her head, and in that moment, she looked a hell of a lot like the Stryx.

I backed up. "Right. Thanks again!"

I turned and ran, but not before I caught sight of the dirt at the edges of the room *moving*. We were surrounded by the ring of earth in the large circular room, and the crumbly black stuff was shifting. Hecate's magic was filling the space. It reeked of rotten vegetables and sulfur, making it hard to breathe.

All around, a loud groaning noise sounded. The dirt in front of the gravestones shifted more. Wait, was that noise coming from *inside* the graves?

"Necromancy," Maximus said.

Oh fates. One of her powers was freaking necromancy.

As soon as the thought formed, a hand shot out of the dirt closest to me. We were almost to the smoke-filled archway that acted as the exit, but we were too slow.

Bodies began climbing out of the graves, half-rotted corpses that clawed their way out of the dirt.

Oh, hell no. Not zombies!

CHAPTER TWELVE

The zombies rose out of the dirt around me, and I shuddered.

I *hated* zombies.

They groaned and staggered toward us, moving quickly. None of those slow, old movie zombies. Nope, these were as fast as humans.

Side by side with Maximus, I sprinted through the smoky archway. Hecate's laugh was the last thing I heard, and it turned my skin to ice.

We spilled out into the huge cavern with the acid lake. It glowed blackly under the diffuse light coming from the ceiling.

"Left!" Maximus shouted.

We ran left, sprinting around the side of the lake. I looked back, spotting the zombies following us from Hecate's lair. There were dozens of them, and they were fast. Their clothes and bodies were in every stage of decay, but all of them seemed to have their eyes.

They watched us, ravenous and evil. Maybe they hadn't been evil in life, but now that Hecate had gotten her claws into them, they definitely were.

And they were gaining on us.

Shit. No way we could fight them all. And they were going to overtake us. They were faster than humans.

We needed to stall them.

I glanced at the lake, and an idea popped into my head.

I reached for Poseidon's magic, letting it fill my chest with bright, sparkling magic. The water called to me, and I commanded it to rise up as a giant wave. As the lake surged upward, I could feel it like it was part of myself. It formed a massive tidal wave, headed straight for the zombies.

The water crashed down on them, and the creatures hissed. As the wave receded, some were sucked into the lake. Others writhed on the ground as the acid ate at their decayed flesh.

"Nice work," Maximus said.

We sprinted faster, and I glanced backward to check on the zombies. My stomach dropped when I spotted a dozen of them climbing to their feet. They were in way worse shape than they had been, but they were still fast.

"They're coming!" I shouted.

Maximus looked back, then drew his sword and shield from the ether. "I've got this."

He turned and sprinted for the zombies, weapon raised. He moved like a train, so fast and strong that he was nearly to them by the time I processed what he was doing.

He reached three zombies first and swung his sword. It was so long and his strike so fierce that he beheaded them all in one fell swoop. I wanted to whoop like I was at a sporting event, but we'd be better served if I actually got into the fight.

I drew my blade from the ether and ran for him. He'd already cut two other zombies off at the waist and was moving on to the others. Before I reached him, three zombies crawled from the water to my left. I spun to face them, but they were fast. One was on me in an instant.

Fear tightened my muscles.

The creature's skin was hanging from its face, and its eyes bulged as it clawed for me. I swung my sword for its arm and took it off. The zombie reached out with its other arm, and I went for the head this time. It toppled to the ground and splatted like a melon.

I'd have gagged if I'd had the time, but another zombie was already on me. I swung for its neck, taking it out easily. The third was harder, coming up so fast that I barely spotted it. The creature reached for my waist, getting its claws hooked into my jeans' pocket.

It yanked, trying to pull me toward it.

No way in hell.

I heaved backward, using all my strength to break away from the monster. My jeans tore, and I watched with horror as a tiny black stone flew out of my pocket and into the air.

I lunged for it, trying to grab it, but a fourth zombie appeared from the side. He was so fast that I hadn't seen him coming. He swung his hand for me, trying to smash his fist into my face.

Instead, he smacked the airborne transport charm, sending it flying into the lake.

It splashed into the middle.

My heart dropped.

Oh fates.

There was no way we could retrieve that.

"Rowan! Watch out!" Maximus's shout snapped me to attention, and I spun, spotting the two zombies as they reached for me.

I lunged out of the way, throwing myself to the ground. I rolled to face them, swinging my sword wildly. I smashed one right through the middle, and two zombie halves landed on either side of me, smacking to the ground with a squishy thud.

The other zombie threw itself onto me. I barely got my legs up at the last minute and kicked it off.

I scrambled to my feet and lunged for the creature on the ground. It was pushing itself upward, and I swung my sword for its neck and took off its head in one clean swoop.

Panting, I stumbled back and searched for more. All of me ached from slamming to the ground. Maximus had just finished off the last zombie and was surrounded by more than a dozen of them, all in pieces on the ground.

"Let's go!" I shouted.

He turned to me, then sprinted forward.

From behind him, Hecate stepped out of the smoke-filled archway. Rage flamed in her eyes, and she raised her hands.

Ah, shit.

Maximus reached me, and I said, "I lost the transport charm in the lake."

At that moment, Hecate's magic swelled and the lake bubbled.

Maximus nodded once. "Let's get out of here and figure it out on the surface."

Something burst from the lake, and Maximus's eyes widened. My heart leapt into my throat as an enormous sea snake rose high. Bright purple scales and green eyes glinted, along with fangs at least three feet long.

"Go!" I shouted.

We raced around the lake, covering the distance in record time. The snake struck for us, but we darted out of the way each time. My muscles burned, and I felt like my feet had wings. I'd never moved so fast in all my life.

We were near the exit when a roar sounded from behind us. I glanced back, spotting four enormous boar-like creatures climbing out of the water. Shaggy fur coved their hulking bodies, and enormous horns protruded from their snouts. They turned their fiery eyes on us.

Then they charged.

Panic gave me speed, and I sprinted through the blue and purple flames that filled the arch. The massive room on the other side was still full of cloaked worshippers, forming a nearly impenetrable barrier between us and the exit.

"Get behind!" Maximus plowed through the crowd, parting them with his sheer bulk.

But we were still too slow. Frantic, I looked back. The crowd had closed in around us, but the monsters were still coming. They had to be.

As if on cue, they burst through the flaming archway. They were easily eight feet tall, towering over the crowd. Shrieks broke out, and the cult members began to run, heading for the sides of the room. There were arches that way, too, that I hadn't noticed. Other exits, no doubt.

We kept heading for the main stairs, though. As the crowd thinned, we could move faster. Unfortunately, so, too, could the hellhogs.

We reached the stairs and sprinted upward. My lungs and legs burned, but I never slowed. Pounding hoofbeats sounded from behind us as they charged up the wide stairs.

Panting, we spilled out into the crossroads. Carriages rolled through the streets, but we sprinted right into the road, dodging the oncoming vehicles.

My heart thundered in my ears as I ran, but the curses of demon carriage drivers sounded through the noise.

When the world went silent and the carriages stopped moving, I nearly stumbled. I would have, if I hadn't been frozen solid, mid run.

All around, the carriages had stopped. I couldn't even hear

the sounds of the hellhogs' hoofbeats. Next to me, Maximus looked like a statue in mid sprint.

What the hell?

Dark magic rolled over me in a heavy wave, and my limbs unfroze. I staggered forward, catching myself. Maximus did the same, but the rest of the world stayed frozen.

"I must say, you're not what I hoped for." The icy, masculine voice came from the left.

I spun, spotting an enormous man sitting upon an ebony throne, right in the middle of the street.

Hades.

He pinned me with his blazing blue eyes as he tapped his golden scepter against his knee.

"I can't say that I had any expectations of you." As the words left my mouth, I remembered the experience with Hecate. "Except that you would be immensely powerful and majestic."

"Laying it on a bit thick, but I appreciate the effort."

I shrugged. "I'm not used to being around gods."

"Well, don't get used to it."

From his tone, he obviously did not like me. "Why did you give me your power if you don't like me?"

"I don't have to like you." His gaze turned somewhat wistful, which was weird as hell on such a scary-looking dude. "Though I admit to hoping that you would embrace it more. I wanted to offer you all the bounties of hell. To allow you to sit next to me on my throne."

Wait, what? "During the months when Persephone isn't here?"

"Precisely. I gave you one of the most powerful gifts in the universe. And you use it, but you don't embrace it. The darkness could have been your kingdom, but you reject it every time."

Um, no thank you. "I don't want to be part of the darkness."

"Clearly not. Your loss. I don't think you're even capable." He shook his head, disgusted.

Briefly, I wondered if he would take his magic back, now that I'd proven myself unworthy of hell.

An immediate sense of loss filled me.

I hadn't liked this power, but I'd come to terms with it. It was worth it for the good it could do. And now that Hades was here, telling me to my face that I was a dark magic failure...

Well, I felt a heck of a lot better.

Failure to him was success to me, and I'd take it.

I just didn't want to lose the death power. Crazy as it was to say, I meant it. And considering all that, I thought it meant I'd come to terms with it.

"I'm sorry, Hades. But I'll do great things with your magic. I promise."

He scoffed. "Perhaps." His gaze ran up and down my form. "You are powerful, at least. That says something."

"Thanks." *I guess.* The tone was so dismissive that I wasn't sure what to make of it. But he seemed done with me, his form already starting to fade as he disappeared.

I stepped forward. "Is there any chance you could help us get out of here? Back to earth, I mean."

"No." He was already deathly bored with us; that was clear. "And those hellhogs are still coming for you."

With that, he disappeared.

Sound and movement blared to life all around. Carriages started moving, demons shouted. And we were standing right in the middle of it all.

Shit.

"Come on." Maximus grabbed my arm and yanked me forward.

I sprinted alongside him, glancing back to see the hellhogs appearing at the top of the stairs leading from Hecate's lair. I turned and ran faster, catching sight of a familiar cloaked figure walking out of a doorway, her arm draped around a woman with pale hair.

I tugged on Maximus's arm. "This way!"

We turned right at the sidewalk and ran toward Mordaca and Aerdeca. Mordaca's eyes widened when she spotted us. Aerdeca stiffened, her beautiful face even paler than normal.

"Are you going home?" I shouted.

Confusion creased Mordaca's brow. "We are."

"Let's go now!" I skidded to a stop in front of her. "Do you have a transport charm? Can we hitch a ride?"

Maximus pointed back toward the hellhogs, which were only about sixty yards away now. "We're in a bit of a hurry due to them."

"Damn it." Mordaca glared at us, then shoved her hand into the pocket of her long cloak. "Come on."

She hurled the transport charm to the ground, then stepped into it with Aerdeca. I gave the hellhogs one last glance—they were only ten yards off now, close enough to smell their fetid breath—then jumped into the portal.

Gratitude welled within me as the ether sucked me in and spit me out in the middle of Aerdeca and Mordaca's workshop. Maximus followed, and I staggered over to the heavy wooden table to lean against it. Hundreds of herbs hung from the ceiling, scenting the room with a lovely aroma. The fire crackled merrily in the hearth.

Mordaca and Aerdeca stared at us.

"Get into trouble?" Aerdeca said, her voice rougher than normal. She looked tired and stressed, and as much as I wanted to ask what the heck she'd been doing in Hades, I didn't.

"You could say that," Maximus said. "But thanks for getting us out of it."

"You didn't bring a transport charm to get out of there?" Mordaca asked.

"There was a bit of a situation with some zombies."

"Not the first time I've heard that," Mordaca said.

Aerdeca chuckled.

"Did you get what you needed from Hecate?" Mordaca asked.

"You talked to *her*?" Aerdeca gave us an impressed look.

"We did. Mostly." I shrugged. "It went downhill at the end, hence the zombies, but overall, success."

"Good work," Mordaca said. "I assume you need to get back to Scotland ASAP?"

"We do," Maximus said. "Do you have a way?"

She turned to the corner of the room near the fire and waved a hand. The air shimmered briefly, then the glamour fell away and a tall mirror was revealed. "You can go through there. It will take you to the Protectorate."

"Oh wow. You have a direct link?" I asked.

"To anywhere." She eyed me up and down. "But you should get going. You look like you're about to fall over from exhaustion."

Now that she mentioned it, I could tell that I was leaning *really* heavily on the table. Not only was I shaking from adrenaline, but the purest exhaustion tugged at me. It'd been so long since I'd slept that I'd forgotten when it last was.

"Yeah, thank you. I do need a nap," I said.

"A twelve-hour one," Aerdeca said.

I doubted I could swing that, but it sounded divine.

Mordaca waved her hands at the mirror. "Go, go. We have our own things to do anyway."

"Thank you." Maximus wrapped an arm around me, supporting me on our short walk toward the mirror.

"Yeah, thanks," I said. "You're the best."

The two of them just smiled mysteriously. I wondered about them as I stepped into the ether, but as soon as it picked me up and spun me through space, I forgot. We had much bigger problems to deal with, after all.

CHAPTER THIRTEEN

When the ether spat us out on the castle lawn, I nearly staggered. Maximus wrapped his arm around me, and I leaned into him.

"Geez, I'm tired." I dropped my head against his side as we walked toward the castle. I moved as fast as I could, but I was majorly dragging.

It was night here, with the moon hanging high in the sky, though I had no idea what time it was. In the distance, the ghostly Pugs of Destruction charged across the lawn, glinting blue and bright.

"With all the adrenaline gone, I think we can finally feel it." Maximus squeezed me close to him.

"I hope Jude is here." I needed to deliver news of what we'd learned, and I was afraid I'd fall asleep if I had to wait.

I pressed my fingers to my comms charm. "Bree? Ana? You here? Is Jude here?"

"I'm here," Ana said. "Jude, too, but Bree is gone."

"Can you get Jude and meet us in the kitchen?"

"Sure thing."

"Oh, and what time is it?"

"Nine."

Not that late, then. We climbed the stairs to the castle, stepping through the massive wooden doors and into the brightly lit entry hall. It was warm and welcoming, smelling of some kind of stew that Hans must have made earlier. My stomach growled loudly, and Maximus chuckled.

Then his stomach growled.

I nudged him, a tired smile tugging at my lips. "Let's go get a bite and fortify ourselves for what's to come."

He nodded, and we hurried down into the kitchen. With the catastrophes were coming so quick that there was no longer time to meet in the Round Room. If we wanted to have an opportunity to talk *and* eat, we'd have to do both at the same time.

When I stepped into the kitchen, I stopped dead still. It was quiet. Empty. What the heck? It was only nine at night. Hans should be here.

But for the first time ever, he wasn't in the kitchen. Neither was his rat, Boris.

I stopped at the base of the stairs, staring into the warmly lit room, and blinked stupidly. "He's not here."

"The cook?"

I nodded. "Hans is always here. With the exception of the very occasional battle, he's *always* here."

A pot of stew steamed on the AGA stove, and the fire was banked low. A horde of juice boxes sat near the massive fridge. But Hans was gone.

"He's on peacekeeping duty in The Vaults." Ana's voice sounded from behind me.

I turned to see my sister coming down the stairs, her blonde hair gleaming in the light of the fire. She looked exhausted, but that was par for the course.

"What do you mean?" I asked.

"Remember the riots I mentioned? They're getting worse. Everyone we can spare is on peacekeeping duty now."

Oh no.

She gestured for us to move farther into the kitchen, and I realized I was blocking the entrance.

I headed over to the stove to get a bowl of stew, my steps dragging. I gestured for Maximus to go first, but he shook his head, refusing to go until I had. I smiled wearily at him, then filled my bowl. She stepped up behind me and filled her bowl once I was done.

I snagged a juice box off the counter and went to sit at the table. Ana and Maximus joined me. I started shoveling food into my mouth far too fast, but I couldn't stop. Not only did it taste savory and divine, I was so famished that I was shaking.

"It's gotten so bad that they've recruited the cook in peace-keeping efforts now?" Maximus shook his head. "That's bad business."

Ana nodded, shoveling stew into her mouth. "Yep. So I hope you guys were successful in finding the Titans."

"Me too," Jude said from the stairs. I turned to look at her, and she looked even more exhausted than Ana did. A tired smile stretched across her face. "We've finished the weakening spell and the binding spell. So if you have their location, we can stop them."

"We've got it. It's an island off the coast of southern Greece." I relayed everything Hecate had told me as she filled her bowl and sat down to join us, including the idea that there was a tunnel leading into the island fortress from underneath, deep below the surface of the ocean.

Jude tapped her chin, starry eyes considering. "I like the sound of this. We have indicators that there is more magic in that area of the world, so that must be the place. Do you trust Hecate?"

I nodded. "She was a bitch, but I didn't think she was lying. Partially because she thought there was no chance we'd succeed."

"Oh, we'll succeed." Jude's eyes turned hard. "They won't beat us in this. And she said that the Titans are actually in charge?"

I nodded. "The Stryx raised them from Tartarus, but I think it was at their command."

"They're immensely powerful, so it makes sense." Jude leaned back in her chair.

"So we need to get started soon," I said. The idea both excited me and exhausted me. I wanted to stop these bastards —*now*. I just wasn't sure I could move.

"Very soon." Jude nodded. "We're going to look into this island. Find its exact location using what you've given us and if there really is a tunnel. We'll probably send out a small team in the morning."

"I want to go," I said.

"You will," Jude said. "You're a student, but we're past that now. There's no denying we need you in this."

"I can help locate the island too," I said.

"No, you can't. You need to sleep. We'll find what we can, then you'll go out with your team."

I frowned, knowing I needed rest but not wanting to quit. I looked at Maximus. He looked pretty freaking tired too. Finally, I nodded, knowing there was nothing else I could say.

We finished eating quickly, then parted ways. I said a quick goodbye to Ana, who was going to find Nix to ask about the island.

Together, Maximus and I went up to my tower flat. The Menacing Menagerie were nowhere to be seen.

Without a word, we fell into bed. I rolled toward him, wanting to say something about how great it'd been to have him at my side in hell. About how I really cared for him. But before I even reached him, my eyes were closed and sleep was tugging at me.

I never got a chance.

～

I woke with a fuzzy head and a weight on my chest that pushed all the air from my lungs.

Groggily, I opened my eyes.

Romeo sat on top of me, staring down into my face. He patted my cheek with his little hand, and as soon as his gaze met mine, he grinned, tiny fangs peeping out.

Good. You're awake. They want you for a meeting.

I scrubbed my hands over my eyes. "Jude?"

Romeo nodded. *Maximus is in the shower. You have ten minutes to meet Jude and the others.*

Ten minutes!

I surged upward, sending Romeo tumbling off me.

Hey!

"Sorry!" I scrambled out of bed, feeling worlds better. Pale morning sunlight gleamed through the windows, and Poppy and Eloise were stretched out on their backs in the warm light.

Maximus stepped out of the bathroom, a too-small towel wrapped around his waist.

I swallowed hard as my body heated. Damn, he looked good. "We're meeting in ten minutes."

"Shite."

"Yeah." I hurried into the shower. "I'll meet you downstairs."

As I hurried past him, he reached out, grabbed me around the waist, and pressed a hot kiss to my lips. It lasted only seconds, but my mind was fuzzy by the time it was done.

He grinned down at me. "See you in a bit."

I swallowed and nodded, struck dumb, then hurried into the bathroom. I finished my shower in record time. Two minutes later, I tugged on my clothes and grabbed a random tube of lipstick off the bathroom vanity. I didn't know what color it was and I didn't care, but I considered it armor and I didn't want to go into battle without it.

I swung by the kitchen to refill my potion belt and bag, then met Maximus by the door, slicking on the lipstick as I walked. I was such a pro that I knew it would go on straight.

"Ready to go save the world?" he asked.

"Always." I turned back to the bedroom where the Menacing Menagerie were still lounging. "Bye, guys! Be ready to go to war. We might be fighting soon!"

I heard some excited chittering and squeaks, which I assumed came primarily from Eloise.

Maximus and I hurried out of my flat and down the hall.

I pressed my comms charm. "Ana? Bree? I was told we're meeting now. But where?"

"Kitchen again," Bree said. "Everyone needs to eat."

Perfect. My stomach was already growling, as if determined to make up for lost time.

The kitchen was crowded when we arrived, though Hans was still gone. Bree and Ana sat at the big round table, along with Cade and Lachlan. Jude, Hedy, Caro, and Nix were there as well, and everyone was scarfing down muffins and coffee.

I hadn't seen the platinum-haired Caro in days, and she looked as tired as everyone else. Her hair was messy, and she raked a hand through it as she looked up at me and grinned.

Jude met my gaze. "No Hans means no hot food, but this should do."

My gaze landed ravenously on the carafe of coffee. "It'll do fabulously."

Maximus and I sat, and I poured us each a cup. I looked

between Jude and Nix. "Well? Did we find the island?"

Jude nodded. "We did indeed. Your tip about the Mage's Star and its distance from land helped us locate it."

Nix leaned forward. "And I've got a contact who can help you find the underwater entrance, if it exists."

My brows rose. "Really?"

"Yeah. You'll like him."

"We've also got a mega-sweet ride," Caro said.

I turned to her. "What is it?"

"A submersible." She grinned widely.

"Like a submarine?" Maximus asked.

"Exactly," Jude said. "Caro, our multitalented water mage, is the pilot. You six are going in it." She pointed to me, Maximus, Ana, Lachlan, Bree, and Cade. "You're all immensely powerful, and we need a small team. You'll be the ones in the sub looking for the underwater entrance. We'll have standby teams in case it's not there, but we're counting on you."

"Where will the standby teams be?" I asked, not wanting them to be close enough to alert the Titans.

"Don't worry," Jude said. "They'll hold off. We'll have them positioned in boats far away. I don't think we can drop in from the top because of a protective spell that forms a dome over the entire fortress, but we'll deal with that when the time comes."

Hedy leaned forward. "As Jude told you last night, we've finished both potions that will help you fight the Titans." She nodded at Lachlan, the Arch Magus and a potions wizard. "You tell her about yours."

Lachlan turned his dark gaze to me. "The weakening spell needs to be deployed first. It's in potion form and we need them to ingest it, but once they do, their magic won't grow any stronger, which has been our main problem. They'll also be physically weaker, and they should be susceptible to the second potion."

"That one will bind them," Hedy said. "It's basically our strongest murder spell. It will immobilize them so that they can't move, and we can throw them back in Tartarus. But if that magic hits anyone who isn't a god or Titan, they're dead."

"At that point, your job is to weaken the defenses on the fortress," Jude said. "We'll send in reinforcements to get the Titans once they're immobilized. The Order is going to help us put them back in Tartarus."

"We still don't know how their magic is growing or what they plan to do with it," Hedy said. "But if we can stop it and get them back into Tartarus, maybe we don't have to worry about it."

Fates, I wanted an answer to that. I leaned back against the chair, my mind whirring. This was a big plan. With a lot of parts.

I prayed I could live up to my end of the bargain.

An hour later, I stood on a bobbing dock on the Greek island of Crete. I had the special potions in my bag, and we were ready to go. The sun shone beautifully on the sparkling blue water, but we'd be under the surface soon, deep in the darkness.

Maximus stood at my side. So did my sisters, Cade, Lachlan, and Nix, the FireSoul. We were a good team. Bree and Ana had the power of the Norse and Celtic gods respectively, and they could kick some serious butt. Maximus was a badass on every level. And so were Cade and Lachlan. As a Celtic god of war, Cade was a great one to have on your side at any time. Lachlan was the Arch Magus—the most powerful mage in the world— and definitely not one to mess with.

Caro was bringing the submersible around from its berth, and we'd load in soon. Nix would introduce us to her contact, then leave.

I turned to look at Nix, who stared off to sea with a blissful expression on her face. "So, we're meeting a giant sea turtle named Nestor here?"

Nix nodded. "That's the one. He helped me out when I was in the realm of the Greek gods, and we became pals. For a Twinkie, he'll do anything."

I couldn't believe that this was our guide, but if it worked, I wasn't going to say no. I looked down at the bag of Twinkies in my hand. The partially hydrogenated treats were apparently Nestor's favorite thing in the entire world, and Nix had told us to bring a bunch of them. Jude had a weakness for the American treats, so Maximus hadn't had to conjure them.

The water rippled in the distance, and Nix leaned forward. "I think that will be him."

The ripples in the water grew larger, and a huge green head finally broke the surface. The turtle was enormous—at least a dozen feet across. His eyes gleamed a brilliant emerald, and his shell was a pale shimmering green.

"Nestor!" Nix waved.

He bobbed his head and swam closer.

"A Greek turtle is named Nestor?" Maximus frowned.

"Don't ask," Nix said. "He's a weirdo, but he's nice and he'll keep his word."

Nestor stopped right in front of the dock, his gaze going between Nix and the Twinkies in my hand. "Phoenix Knight."

"Hey, Nestor. Thanks for coming. We could really use some help."

"Could you now?" A cunning gleam entered his emerald eyes. "The kind of help that could get me some Twinkies?"

"That's exactly the kind of help we need." Nix gestured to me. "Rowan and her friends are looking for the secret underwater entrance to the Titans' fortress on the island of Lektos."

The corners of Nestor's mouth turned down, and his eyes got shifty. "Why the flippins would you want to go *there*?"

"So the entrance does exist?" I asked.

"Does," Nestor said. "But it's a death trap, ever since the Titans showed up. The whole ocean around their island is tainted with dark magic now."

"It'll get worse if we can't sneak in and stop them."

Nestor fidgeted in the water, clearly annoyed and stressed. "It's dangerous."

"We know," Maximus said. "But can you help us?"

Nestor sighed. "You're sure you want to go there?"

"We don't have a choice," I said.

"Everyone has a choice, sugar."

Sugar? What a weird turtle. "Fine. I have a choice, and I choose to take the risk. It'll be worth it. For the world, and for you." I shook the bag of Twinkies to make my point.

"I'm going to need more than that."

Maximus conjured a few in his hands, and the golden cakes gleamed inside their wrappers. "We'll make it worth your while."

Nestor's tongue snuck out to lick his lips. "All my magic, and I still can't get my flippers on Twinkies unless some human gives them to me."

"That's why you're lucky to have me," Nix said. "Along with my winning personality and loyal friendship, I keep you stocked in Twinkies."

Nestor inclined his head. "You have been good to me, Phoenix Knight. For you, I will help these humans."

Maximus tore the wrapping off one and tossed the cake into the air. The turtle lunged out of the water as if he were a great white shark, snagging the Twinkie and then splashing back into the water. I lunged backward, avoiding the spray.

Nestor surfaced a moment later, a contented grin on his face. "I will lead you to the tunnel, but I warn you—it will be dangerous."

"Always is," I said. "But if you can get us into the fortress, we'll pay you handsomely."

Nix pointed into the distance. "Your submersible is almost here."

I turned to look, and spotted the top of the vessel chugging through the water. Caro pulled it up alongside the dock, and the top hatch popped open a few moments later.

Caro emerged from the hatch, a big grin on her face. "Ready to go?"

"We've got our guide." I pointed to Nestor. "That's Nestor."

He bobbed his head.

"Hey, I'm Caro. Good to meet you." Caro grinned at him, then disappeared back into the boat.

I let everyone else climb in first, and turned to Nix. "Thanks again."

"You can do this, Rowan. I know you can." She reached out and squeezed my arm. "Call on us if you need help."

"We will."

I followed my friends into the cramped confines of the submersible, squeezing onto a tiny U-shaped bench that sat in front of a domed window. I sat between Maximus and Bree. All six of us were pressed in like sardines, but at least we had a good view. Nestor flitted around in front of the viewing window, doing loops and showing off. After a moment, I realized that he was spelling a word with his movements.

"Twinkies," Maximus murmured. "That's what he's spelling."

Everyone laughed.

"We'd better be prepared to pay up with those Twinkies, then," Bree said.

"Everyone ready?" Caro asked. She was situated behind a control panel, with a headset over her bright hair.

"Let's do this," I said.

As the submersible sank below the surface, the water grew darker.

"Lights on." Caro flipped a switch that made two massive beams of light cut through the water.

I gripped Maximus's hand, remembering the attack by the hydra in the lake. There were no hydras in the ocean, though, right? Nestor swam in front of us, leading us through the dark sea. Occasionally, a school of fish would flit by.

"Anyone else feeling a bit claustrophobic?" Bree's face was pale.

"Just a bit," I said. "You're probably too used to flying through the wide-open sky."

"You're in good hands with old Bessie here." Caro patted the complicated dash in front of her.

"Bessie?" Maximus asked. "You've named your high-powered submarine after a cow?"

"Well, she's reliable," Caro said.

"That's pretty much the most important quality I can imagine for an underwater death machine," Maximus said.

Caro chuckled.

"Nestor's turning." Cade pointed to the turtle, who was quickly adjusting his trajectory toward the left. Cade tilted his head to look toward the right. "But what's that?"

I blinked, using my extreme vision from Artemis. "Oh crap. It's a great white shark."

The thing had to be twenty-five feet long. Maybe thirty. Way bigger than a normal shark. A megalodon?

But weren't those extinct?

Whatever it was, the giant shark was headed right toward our turtle friend. Nestor might be big, but he was no match for a shark like that. My heart pitched.

If we didn't do something, we'd watch Nestor meet a grisly end.

CHAPTER FOURTEEN

"What are we going to do?" Caro asked. "This thing doesn't have weapons. And we're three hundred feet deep."

Nestor was swimming in a frantic pattern now, trying to evade the shark.

I stared hard at the shark, trying to get a feel for his life force. If I could just use my gift from Artemis...

I closed my eyes and focused on the beast, trying to separate my consciousness from my body and send it to the shark. It took a moment, perhaps because he was cold-blooded. Or maybe because of the water.

Tension sweat dripped down my spine as I tried, until finally, I could see through the shark's eyes.

Whoa.

This looked different. The water was another shade of blue, and I could almost predict where Nestor was going to swim. Worse, I could feel the shark's ravenous desire to eat Nestor. He wasn't particularly hungry, but he loved turtles. Something about the crunchy shell.

Jerk.

Hey! Don't eat that turtle.

The shark's mind jolted. He sensed me within him, but didn't quite know what to make of it.

He resisted the suggestion, swimming faster for Nestor. Panic fluttered at the edges of my mind. This shark wouldn't agree out of the goodness of his heart. He was a predator and Nestor was prey. He didn't feel bad about eating his dinner. Second dinner, in this case, since he definitely didn't feel hungry.

My mind raced for a solution. *Just think, damn it.*

He's poison, I said. *Look how big he is. Totally not natural. Full of growth hormones. It'll give you terrible diarrhea.*

Did sharks get diarrhea?

I could feel the shark's revulsion. So yeah, it seemed like they did. And this guy did *not* like it. He kept swimming, though, determined.

It'll be the worst. You'll probably end up pooping yourself in front of a lady shark.

That did it. I could feel the shark's horror at the idea. Apparently he had a lady he liked, and he did not want to get sick off of turtle in front of her.

The shark turned in an abrupt 180 and started to speed off. He was so fast that it threw my mind into a tailspin.

Where was my body?

I'd lost track of it. The shark was too fast.

Fear exploded within my mind. For the briefest moment, it nearly overtook me. Forcefully, I shoved it back. No way I was going to be hitching a ride with this shark forever.

I calmed my mind and reached out for my body, using my gift over the sea to help locate it. Once I found the submersible —which was really easy to find, given how much it disrupted the ocean—it was easy to find my body.

When I returned, I gasped, opening my eyes.

"What the heck was that?" Ana asked.

"My Artemis power is evolving," I said. "I basically mind-controlled the shark."

"Wow, awesome." She grinned, then pointed to Nestor. "He appreciates it."

The turtle gave us a quick wave with his fin, then kept swimming. My heart thundered as I watched him, and I took slow breaths to calm myself.

Deeper and deeper we went, until the water began to shimmer weirdly.

"What's that?" Cade asked.

The submersible shook and dropped, the current sucking us down. In front of us, Nestor flailed, his fins whirling as he tried to fight the current.

"Where's that coming from?" Bree's voice was high-pitched, one of the few times I'd heard her sound afraid.

My stomach lurched as the sub plunged through the water, going deeper and deeper, out of control.

"I have no idea." Caro's voice was tense. "But the sub is underpowered. It can't fight this."

We had to control the water, but I wasn't strong enough alone. Not for this.

I looked at Ana and Bree. "Together?"

"Gotta try," Bree said.

All three of us had some kind of control over water. Bree had gotten her gift from a Norse water god, whereas Ana had power over the elements. I reached for their hands, gripping them tight, then used my gift.

The power of the ocean slapped into me, tearing a gasp from my throat. The current was so strong that I could feel it inside myself. Whether it was natural or magical, I couldn't tell. But it was insanely strong.

I fought it, trying to calm the ocean. At first, nothing happened. Both of my sisters looked tense and pale. I could feel their magic in the air as they tried to slow the flow of the current.

My muscles ached and my mind felt sluggish as I gave it everything I had. Long seconds passed, and sweat dripped down my spine. Ana and Bree gripped my hands tightly.

The first clue that it was working came when Nestor slowed his frantically spinning fins.

"I think you're getting it," Caro said, her voice strained.

My magic joined with my sisters, and we forced the ocean to stop dragging us into the depths. I was so grateful to have them here with me, all three of us working together. Without them, I'd never have stood a chance.

"We're good," Caro said. "I've got control again."

"Nestor looks better," Maximus said.

I sagged against him, but didn't dare let go of my control over the water. I could still feel it pulling against me, wanting to drag us down.

As Caro steered us through the ocean, following Nestor closely, my sisters and I kept the water calm. When the submersible's lights finally shined on a massive rock wall, gratitude welled within me.

We'd found the island.

"Thank fates," Bree said.

"There, ahead." Cade pointed to the far right of the window.

I leaned over to get a good view, finally spotting a dark hole in the huge rock wall. Nestor seemed to spot it at that moment, too, and he careened for it.

He led us into the dark passage, and Caro expertly steered the vehicle through a tunnel that was covered in incredible rock formations. I let go of my control of the sea—there was no current in here—and dropped my sisters' hands. We shared a grin.

Slowly, Caro drove us through the tunnel. I couldn't help the sense of awe that filled me as we powered through the passage. When it made an abrupt upward turn, Caro expertly changed our course.

Nestor swam up through the tunnel, leading us toward the Titans. As we rose, the water became darker. Almost as if it were polluted.

"The Titans' dark magic," Maximus said.

I shuddered as it seeped into the sub, making the air stink of rot and decay. Without thinking, I gripped Maximus's hand. It seemed that I was doing that a lot these days—reaching for him for comfort.

When the submersible popped up into a darkened cavern, Caro announced, "We're here."

I scrambled to the hatch, then popped the locks and pushed it open. Carefully, I tested the air. It was stale and humid, but breathable. Green light glowed from the ceiling, illuminating the large cavern that was filled with dark water. On one side, there was a ledge. I squinted up at the green light, using Artemis's gift. It looked like some kind of plant life.

"How's it up there?" Caro asked.

"Fine. There's a ledge we can jump out at."

"Roger." She steered the sub toward the ledge.

The vehicle stopped, and I climbed out onto the rock, my friends joining me. Caro followed last and tied the sub off to a little rock outcropping.

I looked around the room. "There's no exit from here that I can see. No wonder she said it'd be hard to reach the Titans."

"I'm going to do some recon higher up in the cavern." Bree's silver wings flared from her back, and she took off into the air.

I turned around to see Nestor floating in the water, staring at us. His emerald eyes blazed through the dark. I grinned at him. "Thanks for the help."

He bobbed his head. "Pay up."

I laughed and strode to him. It didn't take long to hop into the sub and grab the bag of Twinkies. As Bree flew around the top of the cavern looking for an exit, I handed the Twinkies out to my friends.

Cellophane wrapping crinkled as they unwrapped the cakes, and one by one, we threw them into Nestor's mouth. He leapt into the air, snagging them with delicate accuracy.

He looked so happy that my heart warmed.

I glanced at Maximus. "Saving the world can be fun."

He grinned and threw a cake. "Nestor's a good one."

In total, we probably fed him about thirty Twinkies, and by the time he was done, he had a blissed-out expression on his face. I waved at him as he left.

"Hey, guys?" Bree shouted from the ceiling. "I've found our exit, but you're not going to like it."

CHAPTER FIFTEEN

Bree landed gracefully in front of us, folding her silver wings into her back.

"Well, what does the exit look like?" I asked.

"It's *maybe* an exit. I couldn't see where the thing goes. It's basically a rocky tunnel that leads straight upward, so we'll have to wedge ourselves in and climb. If we fall, though..."

"Splat." Ana grimaced. "I freaking hate heights."

"But it's the only way out of here that isn't underwater, correct?" Maximus said.

"Exactly."

"Then we have to try it," Ana said.

I nodded, feeling for her. She *really* hated heights.

"I'll stay with the sub as planned," Caro said.

"Thanks." Just in case we needed an escape route, we couldn't lose the sub. If someone showed up down here, Caro would have to fight them off.

Maximus looked up toward the ceiling. "How will we get up there?"

"I'm strong enough to carry Rowan up," Bree said. "But for you guys, I think Ana and I might tag team it."

"In a pinch, I could manage alone," Ana said. "But you're all so damned heavy."

Lachlan grinned and pulled her close, pressing a kiss to her forehead.

"Here." Maximus's magic swelled as he conjured sets of climbing gear, just like the ones we'd used back at Atlas's fortress. He gave a quick demonstration.

"Safety first." I grinned as I took the harness and equipment. "I'll go first."

Bree held out her hand, and I grabbed it. She pushed off into the air, silver wings carrying us high. My stomach pitched as my feet dangled, and I squeezed my eyes shut for just a second.

"Nearly there," Bree said.

I opened them and looked down. My friends appeared tiny. Maximus stared up at me, his brow furrowed. The others looked up, too, though Caro sat on the ledge talking to Nestor.

"Okay, you'll have to grab that rock outcropping," Bree said.

We were all the way up amongst the strange rock formations on the ceiling. I could see straight up into a dark crevice that glowed with green light from the same stuff that clung to the main cavern walls.

Bree carried me toward a protrusion of rock near the vertical tunnel, and I grabbed on with my free hand. "I'll let go of your other hand, then give your butt a boost."

Since pulling myself up into the tunnel would be the equivalent of a pull-up, I wouldn't say no to that. She let go of my other hand near the same ledge, and I grabbed on. Then she shoved on my butt, and I hauled myself up into the tunnel, wedging myself in the narrow rocky space.

"I've got it!" I said. "You can get the others."

"Be back soon."

I climbed a little farther into the tunnel, hammering in the first spike and hooking off my rope. My friends could hook off to the same safety spots, and if we fell, we'd hopefully avoid the *splat* that Ana had predicted. Safely attached to the wall, I peered down. Ana had shifted into her giant crow form and was helping Bree carry Maximus up. Her dark feathers gleamed under the glowing green light that filled the cavern. Maximus had grabbed onto one of Ana's talons, and his other hand was gripped in Bree's. He wore the harness with the rope coiled at his waist.

I grinned. "Good teamwork, guys!"

"Thanks, Coach!" Bree said.

They got Maximus close enough to grab the rock, and he hauled himself up into the tunnel behind me. *He* didn't need a butt boost. Probably because he looked like he did pull-ups all day long.

"We're going to get started," I said to my sisters, who were headed back down.

"See you up there," Bree said.

I began to climb through the tunnel, my hands slipping on the slimy green plant that glowed with a strange light. Maximus kept pace behind me. At one point, I nearly slipped, but he reached up and stopped me, pressing one big hand firmly to my butt.

"Thanks." Despite the chilly sweat that formed on my skin as I climbed, his touch warmed me. Every ten feet or so, I hammered in more of the safety spikes.

"Any time."

I glanced down to see Ana, Bree, Lachlan, and Cade following us in a line. The tunnel was so narrow that I could only spot parts of them at any one time, but they were all here.

By the time I reached another large room, I was panting. I scrambled out of the tunnel and onto a stone-paved floor, unhooking my harness and ropes. There was no glowing green plant life, so I shook my hand to ignite my lightstone ring. It gleamed golden, and I scanned the space, making sure we were alone. We were, thank fates.

I stood and inspected the large room more closely, looking for an exit. No luck. Just one humongous rock against the wall. Otherwise, it was totally empty.

Maximus climbed out of the tunnel behind me, and I turned to look at him. Grooves were carved in the stone ground leading toward the hole from which we'd climbed. The rest of the team climbed out.

"I think we just climbed through a drain." But for what? There was no water in here.

"This space is no longer used though. And since there are no doors..." He walked to an enormous stone boulder as the others climbed out of the drain. "I think this is the exit."

"Really?" Bree shook her hand to ignite her lightstone ring and frowned as she walked closer to the boulder. "That thing has to weigh tens of thousands of pounds."

Cade strode up to the rock and pressed his hands to it, concentration drawing his brow lower. His dark hair gleamed in the light of our rings.

"What's he looking for?" I asked Bree.

"Probably magic." She pressed her hand to the rock and concentrated, then frowned. "Yep, there's a spell on this rock."

"I think it will sound an alert if the rock is moved," Cade said.

"Crap." I frowned. "How the heck do we remove the spell? We'd have to know what the original incantation was."

"I can break it," Cade said. "Minor spell-breaking is one of my gifts."

My brows rose, and I nodded appreciatively, vaguely remembering something along those lines. "Heck yeah. Let's do it."

I stepped to the side so I could watch him. He pressed his hands to the massive rock, and his magic swelled. It smelled like a storm at sea and sounded like clashing swords. His eyes blazed black, the green drowned out by darkness. His magic changed, filling my head with visions of battle and blood.

Magic snapped on the air, the spell that protected the door breaking.

He stepped back, grinning. "Done."

"How do you do that, exactly?" I asked.

"God of war. Which means god of death, in a sense. Not like the true gods of death, but I have enough power to kill some spells."

"Cool. Now we just need to move this big-ass rock." I looked at Maximus. "Want to give it a try?"

He saluted, then moved to the side of the rock and braced his hands against it.

"One moment." Lachlan stepped forward. "We don't know what's on the other side, so I'll dampen sound. That thing might be loud when it rolls."

Lachlan's magic filled the air, smelling of leather and pine and sounding like distant thunder. Silence descended, and he nodded.

Maximus leaned into the rock and began to push, his muscles bulging and the veins popping. I joined my friends near him, my gaze intent on the moving rock, and reached for a stunner in my potion bag. It took a moment, but the rock began to move, grinding across the floor as Maximus shoved it aside.

He heaved the boulder two feet over, revealing a darkened corridor, then stood back and wiped his brow.

Nothing jumped out at us, but I didn't release the potion bomb.

Maximus entered the dark tunnel slowly, then turned back and whispered, "Stairs."

I followed him, with Bree behind me. The rest lined up behind her, and we crept up the dustiest set of stairs I'd ever seen. The room we entered was empty, though dark magic filled the large space. Misery and death permeated the walls.

I shuddered. *Dungeon.*

It hadn't been used in a while, I didn't think, but it was still horrible.

"There are more stairs over there." Maximus pointed to the far wall.

We followed him to the stairs and began to climb. They were massive stairs, at least three feet tall, and it was a hard climb. At the top, there was a huge door. The handle was at Maximus's shoulder height.

Titan-sized, like the stairs.

Why did they start right here, instead of deeper within the island? Perhaps the Titans didn't realize there was an underground lake with access to their fortress?

Maximus gripped the huge door handle and tried to open it, but it held firm. He turned back. "Locked."

"I've got it," Bree whispered from behind me.

I pressed myself against the wall so she could slip by and trade places with Maximus. She pulled a little pouch from her pocket. Lock-picking tools. When we'd been young and on our own, her skills with a lock had given us many places to sleep. Though all three of us could pick locks, she was the best by far.

It only took a few minutes before she stood. "My tools were almost too small, but done."

Her voice was so low I barely heard it, and I squeezed her arm in acknowledgement. She pushed open the door slowly and peeked out. Clearly satisfied, she exited. Maximus followed, then me. My heart thundered as I stepped into a quiet hallway.

It was absolutely enormous.

I pressed my back against the wall and looked up at the towering ceiling. It had to be a hundred feet high. The hall itself was equally wide, with an enormous carpet covering the length.

Huge chandeliers hung from the ceiling overhead, but they were dark.

"I feel like I've shrunk," I whispered.

"This whole place must have been built for the Titans' size," Maximus murmured.

I nodded as I looked down the hall in each direction. I had no idea which way to go, so I looked at my friends. They read the question in my eyes, and each of them shrugged.

"Left, then," I whispered.

We headed down the hall, creeping silently along. At the end, we reached an enormous door. Maximus pushed it open just slightly, and I peeked out, feeling like a mouse.

It led outdoors, where the day was unnaturally dark. Shouldn't it be bright out? The sun had been shining when we'd left Crete, and it wasn't night yet. I looked up, spotting a dark gray dome of magic.

The protective charm that Jude had mentioned. Of course. No one would be getting in or out without the Titans' permission. The fortress's inner courtyard was enormous, with huge walls surrounding it. There were buildings situated within the space, all looking like they were of ancient Greek construction.

I ducked back in. "It's empty. Totally."

"Can you hear anything?" Maximus asked.

I poked my head back out and listened, using Artemis's gift. After a moment, I caught the sound of chanting. I searched the courtyard, spotting a huge temple to our left. The sound was coming from there. I ducked back in.

"The only sign of life is coming from a temple. Let's head there."

Everyone nodded, and we slipped out of the door, sticking to the shadows as we hurried toward the temple. We had no idea how we were going to get the Titans to consume the weakening potion before we cast the binding spell, but we'd have to figure it out when we got there. It was just impossible to anticipate what would happen in situations like this.

Fortunately, the temple door was open. When I reached it, I peered around the side, catching sight of hundreds of black-cloaked figures. They stood in front of twelve massive statues, and I'd bet big bucks they were statues of the Titans.

The worshippers chanted something, just like the ones at Hecate's lair. But this time, I could understand them. It was in ancient Greek, so my translation probably wasn't perfect, but they were saying something about the Titans being great and mighty.

I frowned and pulled back, looking at Maximus. "Can you conjure us long black cloaks? With hoods."

He nodded and his magic swelled on the air, just slightly. If I hadn't been looking for the signature, I wouldn't have noticed it. As he conjured the cloaks, everyone sneaked a peek into the temple. Finished, he handed the cloaks around, and we slipped them on.

I gestured for everyone to gather in a huddle. The six of us bent inward, and I whispered, "I think we should catch one of them and interrogate him. Maybe we can get a clue about the Titans and make this a little easier."

There was a round of nodding.

Maximus laid a hand on Lachlan's shoulder. "We're fast. We'll grab one and drag them out."

I nodded. Both of them had magically enhanced speed.

"I can shield you," Bree said. "Use a bit of illusion to hide you."

"Once you've got him, we'll meet you in there." I pointed to a nook in the temple wall. It was tucked behind a series of statues and would provide enough cover.

Maximus and Lachlan nodded, then flipped up their hoods and melted into the temple. Bree stood at the entrance, using her magic to hide them. The gift of illusion had come from Loki, and damned if it wasn't handy in situations like this.

"Come on." I grabbed Ana's hand, and we slipped into the little alcove in the wall. Cade joined us.

I waited, muscles tense, until Bree joined us. A few seconds later, Maximus and Lachlan appeared, a cloaked figure held between them. Maximus had his big hand clamped over the man's mouth.

I blinked at the guy, surprised. He looked young. And human. And normal.

What was a guy like that doing here, worshipping the Titans? Looks were deceiving, but still, I'd expected a bunch of miserable demons.

Fates, it must be their black magic. They were influencing more and more people as they grew stronger and their reach increased.

The man glared at me as I reached for my potions belt and withdrew a powerful truth serum. I pulled it out and looked at Lachlan. "You may want to dampen sound."

He nodded, then said, "You're good. We can hear, but anyone outside of our small circle won't notice a thing."

"Perfect." I looked at the guy. "You're going to drink this. It's just truth serum, so it won't hurt you."

He shook his head violently, trying to throw Maximus and Lachlan off of him. It didn't work.

"Fine." I stepped forward and pinched his nose.

His eyes bulged. Maximus released his mouth, and when he opened it to breathe, I poured the potion in. Maximus put his hand back over his mouth.

Finally, the guy's throat moved as he swallowed. Maximus removed his hand.

"Open your mouth," I said.

The guy glared at me. I pinched his nose harder. It was a

little thing, but it worked. The man opened his mouth, and I looked in. No potion. Fantastic.

Also kinda gross.

The things we do to save the world.

"Okay, we have some questions," I said.

He just stared at me, his face set in belligerent lines.

"Where are the Titans now?" I asked.

He pressed his lips together. I just waited, tapping my foot. Slowly, his face turned blue. My potion was a tricky one—you couldn't breathe until you told the truth.

For a second, I thought he might be willing to suffocate to death. And he might have been. Fortunately for us, the human body had such an instinct to survive that I didn't have to worry about that. He'd be forced to talk.

"They're in their quarters," he finally blurted.

"Where's that?" Maximus asked.

"Across the square from here." He pointed to the other side.

"What are they doing?" I asked.

"I don't know." He said that bit immediately, since it was easy.

"Fine. Where are the Stryx?"

"Maybe with them. Maybe in their quarters."

"Where are those?" I asked.

"Next to the Titans'. A few rooms down to the left."

I nodded, deciding immediately to go for the Titans first. As much as I had a vendetta against the Stryx, the Titans were the obvious threat.

"How are the Titans getting so much magic? Why is it expanding like it is?" I asked.

He pursed his lips again, but once more, he turned blue and finally spat out, "They're absorbing all the good magic in the world and turning it dark. It's not *new* magic. It's just transformed magic."

I felt like I'd been punched in the gut. Taking all the good magic?

That would leave us helpless.

It wasn't just that more dark magic was appearing and converting people to evil. It was that they were taking the *good* magic. Oh fates.

"How?" Maximus demanded.

We waited another few moments for him to finally spit it out.

"They don't have to do anything." The man shrugged. "Their hearts are made of pure darkness, and they're so powerful that they absorb it naturally. Once absorbed, it's converted."

So if we could deploy the weakening potion, they'd probably stop absorbing the magic.

"Why do they want all this magic? What are they doing with it?" I demanded.

"They're gaining followers, of course." He pointed to himself. "They want worshippers, and *we want to worship.*"

He said the last bit with such feverish glee that it made me uncomfortable. In all truth, he probably didn't want to worship. He'd been tainted by their dark magic.

"It makes sense," Maximus said. "They were usurped by the Greek gods and thrown into Tartarus. They'd want to resume their rightful place."

"And probably destroy the Greek gods as well, if they could." Bad news for them. Saving all of humanity would come first, but if I managed that, the gods would be saved by default.

I sure hoped they'd known what they were doing when they'd chosen me for this job.

"And what about the Stryx?" Maximus asked. "What do they get out of this?"

"Power." The man shrugged. "Idiots. The Titans probably won't share with them."

He was probably right.

From inside the temple, I heard the voices fade away. I looked at my friends. "I think the service is over."

"Are we done with questions?" Bree asked. "Seems like we got a lot."

I nodded and looked at Maximus.

"Done." He conjured two lines of rope, and bound the man, then gagged him. We left him hidden in the alcove and hurried toward the quarters where we would hopefully find the Titans.

Please let them be there. And please don't let us die.

CHAPTER SIXTEEN

In a silent, single-file line, we crept through the shadows at the edge of the courtyard, heading for the Titans' quarters. We still wore the cloaks, so we could blend in with the worshippers. I wasn't positive which building they were in, but the powerful sense of black magic definitely indicated we were going in the right direction.

When we neared the building that contained the grossest magic, I found another alcove to hide in. We piled in and formed a small circle.

"I think we're close enough to try the invisibility charms." We wouldn't have long with them, so I hadn't wanted to waste them. I looked at Ana. "Do you think they will work?"

"Give me a sec." She closed her eyes, calling on her Druid sense. She had a bit of premonition that normally worked best when asked a direct question. Her eyes popped open. "It's unlikely. They're so powerful they'll see through it."

"Damn." Disappointment twisted within me. "What about illusion?"

Bree could make us invisible with her illusion, but it was more difficult to operate that way. With the potions, we could all see each other as long as we'd drunk the same one. The illusion worked on everyone, however, meaning we couldn't see each other while we worked. That would be bad news for the final part of our mission, when we deployed the binding spell and needed to work in tandem, but it would be useful for the first part.

Ana frowned and closed her eyes. When she opened them, she shook her head. "Same story."

"Okay, so we have to be extra sneaky." I looked at everyone in turn, finding each face set in a determined expression. "Ready?"

Five nods.

I turned and slipped out of the alcove, my friends at my back. The huge building that emitted the darkest magic had an enormous door that was tightly shut.

I frowned. Opening that would be a terrible idea. They'd probably notice.

If only there was an open window. But we'd have to sneak around the entire building to find it.

As if they'd heard my thoughts, the Menacing Menagerie appeared in front of me.

You called? Romeo raised his brows.

I grinned and nodded. "Is there an open window anywhere?"

You're in luck. Follow me.

He turned and scampered away, Eloise and Poppy at his side. I gestured for my friends, and we followed after them, skirting around the building.

Romeo stopped beneath a window and pointed up, a toothy grin on his face. *In there. Real big Titans.*

I rubbed his head and mouthed, "Thanks."

Lachlan was probably already buffering our sound with his magic, but I didn't want to take any chances. I looked up at the window, which was located about twenty feet over my head. The stones that made up the building were rough enough that I could get a few handholds, so I started climbing.

Maximus climbed along beside me, with my sisters and the guys behind. When I reached the sill, I peeked inside.

My stomach dropped.

Holy fates, the Titans were big. Even bigger than when I'd seen them at the gates to Tartarus. Not only was their magic growing, but *they* were growing.

They had to be at least forty feet tall now. Holy fates, they could crush me in their palms.

I swallowed hard.

Don't get caught.

Number one rule.

They were also more human-looking, now. Before, they'd looked like enormous rock-people. As if their time in Tartarus had twisted them. But as their power grew, they appeared to be regaining their old forms. There were two men and one woman. One of the men wore a massive golden crown. Maybe he was Cronus, the king of the Titans. The other man had two massive horns protruding from his head. I couldn't remember which Titan had horns, but I'd bet a bit of research would identify him. The woman had golden hair and blazing yellow eyes, but was otherwise unidentifiable.

For now.

The three of them sat in enormous chairs near a fire, each puffing away at a pipe. Titans of leisure, maybe, though I doubted it. Were they just sitting around and waiting for their magic to grow enough that they could take over the world?

Possibly. It seemed like that was all they *had* to do, anyway.

The windowsill was wide enough that we could all sit on it, and part of it was covered by heavy drapes that would hide us from the Titans' sight.

I scrambled up behind one of the curtains and squished up

against the wall, making room for everyone else. My heart thundered as I waited for them to climb up, and once again, I prayed Lachlan was blocking our sound. My heartbeat was so loud I wouldn't be surprised if the Titans could hear me.

Once we were all crowded onto the sill, with the Menacing Menagerie all crammed onto my lap, Lachlan gave the thumbs-up.

"Okay," I whispered. "I've got a plan. I think." I looked at Lachlan. "The weakening spell that you made—you said it has to be ingested, right?"

"Right."

"Can they smoke it?"

He frowned just briefly as he thought, then nodded. "That'd work. I like how you're thinking."

I grinned and pointed toward the table that sat next to Cronus, the crowned Titan. There was a big pot of tobacco on it. "I'm going to sneak in and pour the weakening potion into the tobacco. Once that's done, get in position to cast the binding spell."

We'd already discussed this. We each had a part to play with that, but we'd need to be positioned strategically around the room to deploy the spell. It was like an energy field that would bind them, but we needed to hit them from all directions for it to work.

Maximus squeezed my hand. "Be careful."

"Always." I rubbed the three little heads of the Menacing Menagerie. "And I've got a distraction if I need one."

The dumpster divers nodded.

"Okay, I'm going." I pressed a quick kiss to Maximus's lips, then squeezed my sisters' shoulders.

The Menagerie disappeared from my lap, and I peered out from behind the curtains, spotting the Titans. They were still smoking away, and staring into space.

Were they smoking tobacco or something else?

I sniffed the air, but it didn't help much. I'd never smoked, and certainly not a pipe, so I couldn't really tell. But there was a chance they were smoking magical hallucinogens to have visions. Plenty of people did it, and the Titan whose eyes I could see the most clearly looked a bit weird.

Holy fates, were they stoned?

That'd be the best gift ever. Slow, stoned villains were the best kind.

Once I determined that none of the Titans were looking right at me, I shimmied down the wall behind the curtain. When I reached the floor, I crouched and peered out from behind the heavy fabric.

The furniture looked huge from down here. The seats of the Titans' chairs were almost twenty feet off the ground. Bree could have flown over and delivered the potion, but then she'd have been at their eye level. Too dangerous. And I could have thrown it into the pot, but there was no guarantee the potion vial would break on impact, since the tobacco wasn't a hard surface.

Carefully, I dug the tiny potion vial out of the zippered pocket of my bag and tucked it in my pocket. I also withdrew the little pot of magical dust for the binding spell. My friends each had identical pots. I shoved that one in my other pocket for later. There was nothing between me and the table with the tobacco, but if I could just get to the base of the chair, I would be out of their eyesight.

When the Titans weren't looking, I sprinted across the floor, my footsteps silent due to Lachlan's magic. My heart nearly burst from my chest when the horned Titan shifted in his chair, but he didn't look down.

Panting, I squeezed myself against Cronus's chair leg, hiding from their sight. Being so close to their dark magic made my skin prickle as if giant spiders were crawling over it.

I shivered, then looked up at the table.

Fates, that's high up.

From down here, I couldn't tell if the Titans were looking at me or not, so I glanced back toward my friends. Bree gave me the thumbs-up, and I tucked the tiny vial into my pocket and began to climb up the table leg. Fortunately, it was intricately carved, which gave me great handholds.

Which I needed, since I was majorly stress-sweating. As I neared the top, it only got worse. This was like climbing into a cage full of hungry alligators, and I did not have iron courage. Though I liked to think of it as a well-developed sense of self-preservation.

When I reached the top of the table, I peered up. My heart thundered. I was so close to Cronus's arm that I could spit on it.

I kind of wanted to.

Nope, dumb.

He was looking into the distance, fortunately. So were the others.

Quickly, I scampered up onto the table. The pot of tobacco was big, but it was still only three feet tall. Not big enough for me to hide behind. There was a big glass, though, and I slipped behind it, crouching down. Carefully, I tugged the little vial of potion out of my pocket and uncorked it.

Only four feet to go to get to the tobacco pot.

I crept out from behind the glass, and one of the Titans shifted toward me.

Shit!

I froze.

A squeaking sound echoed through the room, and the Titan shifted away without seeing me. I caught sight of the Menacing Menagerie standing near the wall.

"Rats," said one of the Titans.

I was briefly offended for my friends, but grateful as hell.

While the Titans glowered at the Menagerie, who scampered away, I raced toward the tobacco and sprinkled the potion in, trying to liberally coat the tobacco.

As soon as I was done, I sprinted back to the table leg and shimmied down. Panting, I tucked myself against the back of the chair.

The Titans hadn't gotten up to chase the Menagerie, which didn't surprise me. Kings didn't chase rodents.

I looked up toward my friends. Bree peeked out and gave the thumbs-up. I hurried back toward the curtain near the wall so I could get a better view.

Tucked behind the curtain, I held my breath as I waited for the Titans to smoke the poisoned tobacco.

When Cronus reached for the tobacco pot, my heart leapt. He refilled his pipe, then his friends'.

And they smoked it.

I wanted to do a little dance as I watched each one inhale the smoke and puff it out.

Jackpot.

Their magic would stop growing. Soon, they'd be weak enough to be susceptible to our binding spell. I looked up toward the windowsill where my friends sat.

Bree was already lowering herself down the wall, followed by Maximus. Cade stayed up there to do his part of the binding spell, but the others joined me on the ground.

Victory and tension shined on my friends' faces. I pointed to Lachlan, then toward the far side of the room. He nodded and went to take up his position. I did the same with everyone else, making sure we were evenly spaced around the Titans. There was a window for each of us to climb onto, fortunately.

I went last, heading to the farthest part of the room. On silent feet, I hurried toward another long set of curtains, tucking myself behind them.

Once I was safely concealed, the Menacing Menagerie appeared. I bent down to whisper to them. "Good job. Now, can you guard the door and let me know if the Stryx come?"

The three nodded, little eyes bright, then disappeared.

Okay, this was it. My heart thundered with excitement and fear as I climbed back up the wall and perched myself on another window. We were lucky that there were so many windows here. The spell would work better if we were up high.

If I looked carefully, I could see the curtains rustling as my friends climbed up. Hopefully the Titans actually *were* high and not very observant.

Once everyone was in place and had given the thumbs-up, I reached for the tiny container of powder that was shoved in my pocket. When combined with the right incantation, this would bind the Titans tightly.

I opened the little container and held my breath, not wanting to ingest any of it. The powder itself wasn't supposed to be deadly—it needed the incantation to turn it into something that would kill a human in a heartbeat. Still, I didn't want to take any chances. I counted to thirty to give my friends a chance to get ready, then stepped out from behind the curtain, the little container held in front of my face.

Maximus, Bree, Ana, Cade, and Lachlan all stepped out from behind their curtains.

Go time.

I blew on the powder, sending it flying into the air. My friends did the same, and the glittery potion sparkled in the light.

I caught the gaze of one of the horned Titans, and fear iced down my spine. There was no time to hesitate, though. I raised my hand and sliced it down, the signal to start the incantation.

"Of myth and dark, we give the spark. Binding three, our will shall be." Everyone spoke in unison, imbuing the powder with magic. It lit up a brilliant blue, forming streaks of blue lightning that caged the Titans in a glowing dome.

It was weak, though, and the Titans surged to their feet, anger creasing their faces.

"Of myth and dark, we give the spark. Binding three, our will shall be." We kept chanting, giving the binding spell power. It'd need more time, though. Lots more.

Which made this the hard part.

Panic exploded within me as the Titans roared in unison. Cronus raised his hands, and dark magic filled the air. While the binding spell was still growing in strength, the Titans would be able to fight.

We'd just have to hold them off until we were finished.

The Titan sliced his hand toward me, and the stone windowsill upon which I stood shattered. The stones tumbled, and I fell, my stomach jumping into my throat.

At the last second, I caught the stone ledge, dangling. My voice became squeaky, but I never stopped chanting, keeping it up as I scrambled down to the ground. My friends' voices filled the air, loud and sure. Now that we'd started the spell, we could move around. We just couldn't stop the chant. The words helped our own magic give the powdery potion strength, and with Titans this big, the spell needed all the power it could get.

Once on the ground, I turned to face the Titans. My heartbeat roared in my head as I braced myself for attack. Bree flew through the air above their heads, distracting the horned Titan. He shot massive bolts of lightning at her, but she dodged them elegantly, chanting all the while. The thunder that accompanied the lightning made my head hurt like hell. She was careful not to touch the glowing blue light that caged them, however. If any of us touched it, we'd be dead.

The Titan who'd broken my windowsill flung out his hand toward Maximus, shattering the sill upon which he stood.

Maximus leapt gracefully to the ground and landed in a crouch as the stone tumbled down behind him.

"Of myth and dark, we give the spark. Binding three, our will shall be." The words echoed through the room as the same Titan broke Ana's windowsill. The entire room shook from the force of his power, and I stumbled to my knees. Ana fell, not daring to take on her crow form since then she couldn't chant. At the last minute, Lachlan caught her.

If he kept that up, he'd bring down the building around us. It was already half full of rubble.

The third Titan roared, her eyes shooting flames that barreled into the curtains by Cade. He leapt off the window and swung down to the ground using the drapes. Smoke filled the air as the Titan lit up all the textiles, and the heat made my skin burn.

The Titans were trapped, but they weren't down. Not even close.

Oh fates, we could die before we finished this.

I shouted the chant, and the blue light of the binding spell grew brighter. Next to me, the wall exploded, sending a huge chunk of rock right into my side. I plowed into the ground, pain flaring as the words were forced from my lungs. I gasped, trying to catch my breath and start the chant again.

Broken ribs.

The pain was sharp, making it hard to speak, but I kept it up. In agony, I climbed to my feet.

At this rate, we weren't going to succeed. We could barely fight back since we couldn't touch the blue light.

I needed something that would hurt them from afar.

Lightning.

Except, when Bree had thrown lightning at one of them during the last battle, he'd just laughed as he'd absorbed it. I needed something good and pure to throw at them. And strong. Something they would hate.

Warmth began to fill me, as if responding to my need. It glowed through my limbs, as hot as the sun. All around, the room glowed brighter.

Wait, was that coming from *me?*

Hit them.

I blinked, hearing the voice in my head.

I was getting a new power.

Blind them. Use the sun.

Sunlight. Somehow, I'd been given the power of sunlight. It filled my soul with brightness. Battle exploded around me as I raised my hands, calling upon the new magic.

Then I hesitated.

No. I couldn't just hit them with light. It needed to be more than that. They were evil and I was not. No matter the darkness within me, I chose differently for myself. I chose good.

So I called on all the goodness within my soul. Whatever kindness and generosity I possessed, I tried to stuff it into the sunlight within me. It was a weird process—and I had no idea if I was doing it right—but I imbued the sun magic with my own light.

Then I raised my hands and shot it right at the Titans, keeping up the chant the whole time. The light blasted from me, so bright white that I couldn't see.

The Titans roared, sounds of rage and pain. The light dimmed, turning from white to a bright, golden yellow. I could see again, and the Titans were lit up like gold Christmas tree lights. They stood frozen still, my light and goodness binding them.

My friends, all of whom looked like hell, shouted the chant even louder, their words filling the room along with the smoke.

The blue cage grew brighter and smaller, shrinking to wrap around the Titans.

We were nearly there!

I shouted the chant, continuing to send my light into the Titans. It froze them solid, and if we were lucky, we'd finish the binding before we died in their apocalyptic sitting room. We were almost there. So close.

Romeo appeared in front of me, pointing to the door. *Incoming!*

My gaze widened as I turned to look. The Stryx charged into the room, their purple eyes wide with horror. Their black hair floated around their heads, and they spun to search the room.

I didn't dare let up on the sunlight that bound the Titans, but my friends charged the Stryx. One of them turned to Maximus, raising her hands. She threw a bolt of lightning at him, but he dodged it, sprinting right for her, continuing to chant the whole while.

He plowed into her, taking her down to the ground.

The others converged on the second Stryx. They'd be on her any second, too many for her to fight. Her head flew as she looked at each of them, then a determined glint entered her eyes.

Oh, shit.

I didn't know what that meant, but I didn't like it.

She raised her hand and threw a single blast of lightning, right at Maximus. It blew him off her sister.

Before the others reached her, she shouted, "For the Titans!"

Then she charged into the blue light of the cage. It caught her, holding her within the light, her body lighting up like a cartoon of someone being electrocuted. Her sister followed, throwing herself into the light as well.

They began to chant, shouting their own spell.

What the hell?

Then I caught the words.

"Unto me, I take the spell from thee!" Over and over, they repeated it, their voices shrieking over the roar of flames that enveloped the room.

It worked quickly, and the blue light faded from the Titans, flowing into the Stryx.

Holy fates, they were killing themselves.

To save the Titans.

Horror opened a hole in my chest.

The last of the blue light flowed into the Stryx, who glowed such a bright blue that I could no longer see their human forms. Then they exploded, poofing away in a blast of blue light.

Rage and fear fought a battle within me. We'd failed.

There was no time to mourn, or we'd all die.

I turned to the Titans, throwing every last bit of goodness and sunlight that I could manage. It exploded out of me again as a bright white light, stronger than ever before. I dropped to my knees, so weak I couldn't stand.

Looking at the three Titans was like looking at a trio of suns. My magic was too much for them. But how much did I have?

I kept pushing it toward them, eventually falling onto my hands, unable to stay on my knees.

The three Titan-suns moved toward each other and smashed together.

Then they disappeared.

I collapsed, too weak to move.

Shit.

They'd run.

We'd failed.

And the room was going up in flames all around us. Wracking coughs tore through my chest as I tried to stand, to escape. But I couldn't. I'd used up everything, and I was too weak to move. Rubble and smoke surrounded me. Where were my friends? Were they alive?

"Rowan!" Bree and Ana screamed.

"I've got her!" Maximus's shout cut through the smoke, then strong hands grabbed me and pulled me up. He cradled me to his chest and sprinted through the smoke, leaping over piles of rubble. My broken ribs ached, but I didn't care as long as he got me out of here.

"Is everyone okay?" I coughed.

"Yes." He sprinted faster, racing into the cool air of the outdoors. I sucked it into my lungs, looking around frantically for everyone else.

I spotted the Menagerie first, looking charred and smoky, but fine. Ana and Bree stood next to Lachlan and Cade, and they all looked like hell. Ana's arm hung at a weird angle, clearly broken, and blood poured down Bree's face. Cade was leaning heavily on one leg, while Lachlan had a nasty burn on his shoulder.

Slowly, the worshippers left the temple and stared at us, standing in a circle. When Maximus turned to look at them, they shrank back like frightened rabbits.

We'd driven off their Titans. They might be pissed, but they were afraid of our power.

Good.

I dropped my head against Maximus's shoulder and looked at my team. "We failed."

"No, we didn't." Bree shook her head. "We took out the Stryx."

"And we permanently weakened the Titans," Ana added.

Cade grinned. "We learned what their final goal is. And now that we've seen them, we can probably identify them. Find their weaknesses."

"And we destroyed their headquarters," Lachlan said.

Maximus met my gaze. "We know that they're terrified of you."

I looked up. "Terrified?"

"They ran like cowards. They know you can kill them."

I nodded, gritting my teeth. Determination flowed through me. I could kill them. I *would*.

For the world, I had to.

EPILOGUE

The next day, my ribs were finally healed. It'd taken a powerful healing tonic from Hedy, but I was feeling tip-top. Mostly.

Everyone else was healed as well, thank fates. There'd been some nasty injuries, and it'd been a miserable journey back through the fortress to get to Caro and the sub, but we were all better.

I leaned back on my couch, closing my eyes.

An hour ago, we'd finished our meeting with Jude. Though I felt the sting of failure over our mission, Jude had agreed with everyone else. It had been a success. Mostly because we'd permanently weakened the Titans and destroyed the Stryx. Defeating such insane evil was usually a multi-step process, she'd said. We knew who they were, too. I'd been right about the crowned one being Cronus. The horned one was probably Crius, whose name meant *ram*. And the one who shot flames from her eyes was Theia, Titan goddess of shining. Which was weird, but if it allowed her to shoot flames from her eyes, that was freaking bad ass.

And we now had a weapon to use against them.

Me.

I figured it was Apollo who'd given me the sun magic, and I was determined to practice until I could make a nuclear blast that would destroy them for good. We just had to find them again.

We suspected that wouldn't be quite as hard this time. With their special fortress destroyed—we'd bombed the hell out of it after evacuating the worshippers—their dark magic would be easier to track.

A knock sounded at my door, and I blinked my eyes open. It was ten o'clock. I was supposed to be in bed soon.

"Yeah?" I called as I stood.

"It's Maximus."

I grinned, unable to help myself. After the meeting, he'd disappeared immediately. He hadn't even said goodbye, which I thought was weird.

I opened the door, gasping at the sight of a huge cluster of roses. Maximus held them out, along with a picnic basket and a bottle of wine.

I took the basket and the roses, stepping back into the room. "What's all this?"

"Our date."

I smiled and let him in, then shut the door. "I don't recall scheduling a date."

"That's because it never works when we schedule. And since we'll be off hunting the Titans tomorrow morning, I figured we'd better take the time now."

I grinned. "You brought a picnic?"

"We'll go out for a real date once we've defeated the Titans."

"This *is* a real date." I set the flowers and picnic basket on the counter, then grabbed the wine from him and set it down, too.

I turned away from it, facing him. He looked so damned good in his dark T-shirt and jeans. Strong and tall, and handsome as sin. My fallen angel.

"Not a fan of the food?" he asked.

"Not right now. I have something better in mind." I moved toward him, wrapping my arms around his neck and leaning up to press my lips to his. The scent of cedar rushed over me, and I drew it in.

He groaned and pulled me toward him, pressing me full length against his body. I reveled in his strength as I kissed him.

Pleasure streaked down my body, and I shivered. He ran a series of kisses down my neck, sending electricity through my veins. When he picked me up, I wrapped my legs around him, touching every inch that I could. He was hard everywhere, and I couldn't get enough.

"Want to take me upstairs?" I whispered against his lips.

"I couldn't possibly want anything more."

Funny thing was, neither could I.

THANK YOU FOR READING!

I hope you enjoyed reading this book as much as I enjoyed writing it. Reviews are *so* helpful to authors. I really appreciate all reviews, both positive and negative. If you want to leave one, you can do so on Amazon or GoodReads.

Join my mailing list at www.linseyhall.com/subscribe to stay updated and to get a free ebook copy of *Death Valley Magic,* the story of the Dragon God's early adventures. Turn the page for an excerpt.

EXCERPT OF DEATH VALLEY MAGIC

Death Valley Junction
Eight years before the events in Undercover Magic

Getting fired sucked. Especially when it was from a place as crappy as the Death's Door Saloon.

"Don't let the door hit you on the way out," my ex-boss said.

"Screw you, Don." I flipped him the bird and strode out into the sunlight that never gave Death Valley a break.

The door slammed behind me as I shoved on my sunglasses and stomped down the boardwalk with my hands stuffed in my pockets.

What was I going to tell my sisters? We *needed* this job.

There were roughly zero freaking jobs available in this postage stamp town, and I'd just given one up because I wouldn't let the old timers pinch me on the butt when I brought them their beer.

Good going, Ana.

I kicked the dust on the ground and quickened my pace toward home, wondering if Bree and Rowan had heard from Uncle Joe yet. He wasn't blood family—we had none of that left besides each other—but he was the closest thing to it and he'd been missing for three days.

Three days was a lifetime when you were crossing Death Valley. Uncle Joe made the perilous trip about once a month, delivering outlaws to Hider's Haven. It was a dangerous trip on the best of days. But he should have been back by now.

Worry tugged at me as I made the short walk home. Death Valley Junction was a nothing town in the middle of Death Valley, the only all-supernatural city for hundreds of miles. It looked like it was right out of the old west, with low-slung wooden buildings, swinging saloon doors, and boardwalks stretching along the dirt roads.

Our house was at the end of town, a ramshackle thing that had last been repaired in the 1950s. As usual, Bree and Rowan were outside, working on the buggy. The buggy was a monster truck, the type of vehicle used to cross the valley, and it was our pride and joy.

Bree's sturdy boots stuck out from underneath the front of the truck, and Rowan was at the side, painting Ravener poison onto the spikes that protruded from the doors.

"Hey, guys."

Rowan turned. Confusion flashed in her green eyes, and she shoved her black hair back from her cheek. "Oh hell. What happened?"

"Fired." I looked down. "Sorry."

Bree rolled out from under the car. Her dark hair glinted in the sun as she stood, and grease dotted her skin where it was revealed by the strappy brown leather top she wore. We all wore the same style, since it was suited to the climate.

She squinted up at me. "I told you that you should have left that job a long time ago."

"I know. But we needed the money to get the buggy up and running."

She shook her head. "Always the practical one."

"I'll take that as a compliment. Any word from Uncle Joe?"

"Nope." Bree flicked the little crystal she wore around her neck. "He still hasn't activated his panic charm, but he should have been home days ago."

Worry clutched in my stomach. "What if he's wounded and can't activate the charm?"

Months ago, we'd forced him to start wearing the charm. He'd refused initially, saying it didn't matter if we knew he was in trouble. It was too dangerous for us to cross the valley to get him.

But that meant just leaving him. And that was crap, obviously.

We might be young, but we were tough. And we had the buggy. True, we'd never made a trip across, and the truck was only now in working order. But we were gearing up for it. We wanted to join Uncle Joe in the business of transporting outlaws across the valley to Hider's Haven.

He was the only one in the whole town brave enough to make the trip, but he was getting old and we wanted to take over for him. The pay was good. Even better, I wouldn't have to let anyone pinch me on the butt.

There weren't a lot of jobs for girls on the run. We could only be paid under the table, which made it hard.

"Even if he was wounded, Uncle Joe would find a way to activate the charm," Bree said.

As if he'd heard her, the charm around Bree's neck lit up, golden and bright.

She looked down, eyes widening. "Holy fates."

Panic sliced through me. My gaze met hers, then darted to Rowan's. Worry glinted in both their eyes.

"We have to go," Rowan said.

I nodded, my mind racing. This was *real*. We'd only ever

talked about crossing the valley. Planned and planned and planned.

But this was *go time*.

"Is the buggy ready?" I asked.

"As ready as it'll ever be," Rowan said.

My gaze traced over it. The truck was a hulking beast, with huge, sturdy tires and platforms built over the front hood and the back. We'd only ever heard stories of the monsters out in Death Valley, but we needed a place from which to fight them and the platforms should do the job. The huge spikes on the sides would help, but we'd be responsible for fending off most of the monsters.

All of the cars in Death Valley Junction looked like something out of *Mad Max*, but ours was one of the few that had been built to cross the valley.

At least, we hoped it could cross.

We had some magic to help us out, at least. I could create shields, Bree could shoot sonic booms, and Rowan could move things with her mind.

Rowan's gaze drifted to the sun that was high in the sky. "Not the best time to go, but I don't see how we have a choice."

I nodded. No one wanted to cross the valley in the day. According to Uncle Joe, it was the most dangerous of all. But things must be really bad if he'd pressed the button now.

He was probably hoping we were smart enough to wait to cross.

We weren't.

"Let's get dressed and go." I hurried up the creaky front steps and into the ramshackle house.

It didn't take long to dig through my meager possessions and find the leather pants and strappy top that would be my fight wear for out in the valley. It was too hot for anything more, though night would bring the cold.

Daggers were my preferred weapon—mostly since they were cheaper than swords and I had good aim with anything small and pointy. I shoved as many as I could into the little pockets built into the outside of my boots and pants. A small duffel full of daggers completed my arsenal.

I grabbed a leather jacket and the sand goggles that I'd gotten second hand, then ran out of the room. I nearly collided with Bree, whose blue eyes were bright with worry.

"We can do this," I said.

She nodded. "You're right. It's been our plan all along."

I swallowed hard, mind racing with all the things that could go wrong. The valley was full of monsters and dangerous challenges—and according to Uncle Joe, they changed every day. We had no idea what would be coming at us, but we couldn't turn back.

Not with Uncle Joe on the other side.

We swung by the kitchen to grab jugs of water and some food, then hurried out of the house. Rowan was already in the driver's seat, ready to go. Her sand goggles were pushed up on her head, and her leather top looked like armor.

"Get a move on!" she shouted.

I raced to the truck and scrambled up onto the back platform. Though I could open the side door, I was still wary of the Ravener poison Rowan had painted onto the spikes. It would paralyze me for twenty-four hours, and that was the last thing we needed.

Bree scrambled up to join me, and we tossed the supplies onto the floorboard of the back seat, then joined Rowan in the front, sitting on the long bench.

She cranked the engine, which grumbled and roared, then pulled away from the house.

"Holy crap, it's happening." Excitement and fear shivered across my skin.

Worry was a familiar foe. I'd been worried my whole life. Worried about hiding from the unknown people who hunted us. Worried about paying the bills. Worried about my sisters. But it'd never done me any good. So I shoved aside my fear for Uncle Joe and focused on what was ahead.

The wind tore through my hair as Rowan drove away from Death Valley Junction, cutting across the desert floor as the sun blazed down. I shielded my eyes, scouting the mountains ahead. The range rose tall, cast in shadows of gray and beige.

Bree pointed to a path that had been worn through the scrubby ground. "Try here!"

Rowan turned right, and the buggy cut toward the mountains. There was a parallel valley—the *real* Death Valley— that only supernaturals could access. That was what we had to cross.

Rowan drove straight for one of the shallower inclines, slowing the buggy as it climbed up the mountain. The big tires dug into the ground, and I prayed they'd hold up. We'd built most of the buggy from secondhand stuff, and there was no telling what was going to give out first.

The three of us leaned forward as we neared the top, and I swore I could hear our heartbeats pounding in unison. When we crested the ridge and spotted the valley spread out below us, my breath caught.

It was beautiful. And terrifying. The long valley had to be at least a hundred miles long and several miles wide. Different colors swirled across the ground, looking like they simmered with heat.

Danger cloaked the place, dark magic that made my skin crawl.

"Welcome to hell," Bree muttered.

"I kinda like it," I said. "It's terrifying but..."

"Awesome," Rowan said.

"You are both nuts," Bree said. "Now drive us down there. I'm ready to fight some monsters."

Rowan saluted and pulled the buggy over the mountain ridge, then navigated her way down the mountainside.

"I wonder what will hit us first?" My heart raced at the thought.

"Could be anything," Bree said. "Bad Water has monsters, kaleidoscope dunes has all kinds of crazy shit, and the arches could be trouble."

We were at least a hundred miles from Hider's Haven, though Uncle Joe said the distances could change sometimes. Anything could come at us in that amount of time.

Rowan pulled the buggy onto the flat ground.

"I'll take the back." I undid my seatbelt and scrambled up onto the back platform.

Bree climbed onto the front platform, carrying her sword.

"Hang on tight!" Rowan cried.

I gripped the safety railing that we'd installed on the back platform and crouched to keep my balance. She hit the gas, and the buggy jumped forward.

Rowan laughed like a loon and drove us straight into hell.

Up ahead, the ground shimmered in the sun, glowing silver.

"What do you think that is?" Rowan called.

"I don't know," I shouted. "Go around!"

She turned left, trying to cut around the reflective ground, but the silver just extended into our path, growing wider and wider. Death Valley moving to accommodate us.

Moving to trap us.

Then the silver raced toward us, stretching across the ground.

There was no way around.

"You're going to have to drive over it!" I shouted.

She hit the gas harder, and the buggy sped up. The reflective surface glinted in the sun, and as the tires passed over it, water kicked up from the wheels.

"It's the Bad Water!" I cried.

The old salt lake was sometimes dried up, sometimes not. But it wasn't supposed to be deep. Six inches, max. Right?

Please be right, Uncle Joe.

Rowan sped over the water, the buggy's tires sending up silver spray that sparkled in the sunlight. It smelled like rotten eggs, and I gagged, then breathed shallowly through my mouth.

Magic always had a signature—taste, smell, sound. Something that lit up one of the five senses. Maybe more.

And a rotten egg stink was bad news. That meant dark magic.

Tension fizzed across my skin as we drove through the Bad Water. On either side of the car, water sprayed up from the wheels in a dazzling display that belied the danger of the situation. By the time the explosion came, I was strung so tight that I almost leapt off the platform.

The monster was as wide as the buggy, but so long that I couldn't see where it began or ended. It was a massive sea creature with fangs as long as my arm and brilliant blue eyes. Silver scales were the same color as the water, which was still only six inches deep, thank fates.

Magic propelled the monster, who circled our vehicle, his body glinting in the sun. He had to be a hundred feet long, with black wings and claws. He climbed on the ground and leapt into the air, slithering around as he examined us.

"It's the Unhcegila!" Bree cried from the front.

Shit.

Uncle Joe had told us about the Unhcegila—a terrifying water monster from Dakota and Lakota Sioux legends.

Except it was real, as all good legends were. And it occasionally appeared when the Bad Water wasn't dried up. It only needed a few inches to appear.

Looked like it was our lucky day.

~~~

Join my mailing list at www.linseyhall.com/subscribe to continue the adventure and get a free ebook copy of *Death Valley Magic*. No spam and you can leave anytime!

AUTHOR'S NOTE

Thank you for reading *Threat of Magic!* If you've made it this far, you've probably read some of my previous books and know that I like to include historical places and mythological elements in my stories. Sometimes the history of these things is so interesting that I want to share more, and I like to do it in the Author's Note instead of the story itself.

Threat of Magic was full of mythological elements because we have so much information available about the Greeks and their religion. Many of those elements were as I presented them in the story, but some were modified.

The most obvious modification is the Titans. In the myths, they aren't inherently evil as I present them to be in this story. And likewise, the Greek gods weren't necessarily good. In fact, in many cases, the Greek gods were jerks. For example, Daphne's story of how she ended up in the tree is accurate to myth. In fact, there are many stories where the women get the bad end of the deal.

Anatlia, the realm of the Greek gods, is total fiction. I invented it for Nix's series. However, most of the qualities of the realms within Hades were taken almost directly from primary sources.

There are no sources that I could find that reference the Stryx as worshipping Hecate. Though Hecate does dwell in the underworld alongside Persephone, she does not have her own horrible realm as I presented it.

When Rowan and Maximus entered Hades through the bottomless Alcyonian Lake at Lerna, they spotted a three headed Hydra underwater. This was a reference to the famous Hydra that Hercules fought during his famous labors. The Alcyonian Lake is considered to be one of the entrances to Hades, and the Hydra lived in that lake until Hercules killed it. The Hydra that Rowan and Maximus encountered was a descendent, and I like to think that it was a younger one as it had fewer heads.

I think that's it for the history and mythology in *Threat of Magic*—at least the big things. I hope you enjoyed the book and will come back for more of Rowan, Maximus, Ana and Bree!

To Lisa and Rick, with love.

ACKNOWLEDGMENTS

Thank you, Ben, for everything. There would be no books without you.

Thank you to Jena O'Connor and Lindsey Loucks for your excellent editing. The book is immensely better because of you!

Thank you to Orina Kafe for the beautiful cover art. Thank you to Collette Markwardt for allowing me to borrow the Pugs of Destruction, who are real dogs named Chaos, Havoc, and Ruckus. They were all adopted from rescue agencies.

ABOUT LINSEY

Before becoming a writer, Linsey Hall was a nautical archaeologist who studied shipwrecks from Hawaii and the Yukon to the UK and the Mediterranean. She credits fantasy and historical romances with her love of history and her career as an archaeologist. After a decade of tromping around the globe in search of old bits of stuff that people left lying about, she settled down and started penning her own romance novels. Her Dragon's Gift series draws upon her love of history and the paranormal elements that she can't help but include.

COPYRIGHT

This is a work of fiction. All reference to events, persons, and locale are used fictitiously, except where documented in historical record. Names, characters, and places are products of the author's imagination, and any resemblance to actual events, locales, or persons, living or dead, is coincidental.
Copyright 2018 by Linsey Hall
Published by Bonnie Doon Press LLC
All rights reserved, including the right of reproduction in whole or in part in any form, except in instances of quotation used in critical articles or book review. Where such permission is sufficient, the author grants the right to strip any DRM which may be applied to this work.
Linsey@LinseyHall.com
www.LinseyHall.com
https://www.facebook.com/LinseyHallAuthor

52290308R00129

Made in the USA
Columbia, SC
01 March 2019